SEE
JANE
RUN

SEE JANE RUN

HANNAH JAYNE

sourcebooks
fire

Published by Sourcebooks Fire, an imprint of Sourcebooks, Inc.

P.O. Box 4410, Naperville, Illinois 60567-4410

(630) 961-3900

Fax: (630) 961-2168

teenfire.sourcebooks.com

Library of Congress Cataloging-in-Publication data is on file with the publisher.

Printed and bound in the United States of America.

VP 10 9 8 7 6 5 4 3 2 1

To my father, because this is the book he wanted to read. Thanks for making me take chances.

ONE

"No, Riley. No way."

"But, Dad, you haven't even heard—"

Riley Spencer's father took a slurping sip from his coffee cup and looked over the rim at his daughter. "I said no. End of discussion."

Riley blew out a sigh and crossed the kitchen, slamming the cupboard door after retrieving a coffee cup.

"I hope you're pouring that for me," her mother said, coming up over her shoulder and slipping the now-full cup out of Riley's hands. "What's going on?"

Riley fumed. "I can't go on the school trip—the school trip to look at *colleges*—and now I can't even drink a cup of coffee! It's like you want to keep me here in this stupid little fortress forever!"

Riley's parents were staring at her, her father in mid-sip with newspaper in one hand, her mother with a glint of a half-smile on her pale pink lips.

"Ry, we talked about this."

"No," Riley said, "*we* did not talk about this. *You* talked about this. And no one said I couldn't drink coffee."

Her father shrugged and went back to his paper. "Have a cup of coffee. Be five foot two for the rest of your life. See if I care."

"We already had this discussion, hon. Your father and I said no." Riley saw her mother's eyes flash over the rim of her coffee cup. She gave a quick glance at her husband, and Riley knew she was shut out.

Her mother sighed. "It's not like we do this for no reason, Ry." She shook a single pill from the prescription bottle and held it in her palm. "There will be crowds and a lot of confusion. Dr. Morley said it would be best to ease into a new environment."

Riley glared at the tiny pill before snatching it up and popping it into her mouth. "What's the point of taking antianxiety medication if I never even have the opportunity to get anxious?" But even as she said the words, a tiny, singeing panic burned up the back of her neck. "It's not like I have a panic attack every time I leave the house or anything."

"Riley…"

She slumped, glaring through lowered lashes at each of her parents. She let out a low, dejected sigh before pushing around the cereal in her bowl.

"Well, I guess getting straight As doesn't matter anymore anyway. If I can't even go check out a university on a heavily chaperoned school-sponsored trip, there's no reason to even apply to college. I mean, I don't want to go to a school I've never even visited. Even if it is my beloved father's alma mater. What if there are rapists and murderers surrounding the campus? I'd be caught totally off guard. I guess it's going to be Crescent City Junior College after all. I hear they have a pretty decent math department. I think it was ranked eighty-fifth in America's Best Junior Colleges. Eighty-fifth. That's not bad, right?"

"Ry, we agreed that your dad and I would take you and Shelby to look at colleges over your spring break. What happened to that?"

Riley looked her mother full in the face and blinked. "I have a thirst for knowledge that can't wait, Mom."

A beat passed as her parents shared an is-she-serious look.

"Oh, come on!" Riley moaned.

"Ry, honey." Her mother patted her hand. "We need to make sure you're taken care of. We just like to know you're safe." She offered Riley a tight-lipped smile.

"I'll be safe. You can call me every five minutes. You can shoot one of those pet tracker chips in the back of my neck!"

Her father cocked his head, but he didn't look about to relent. Riley's lower lip started to quiver. She hadn't planned on pulling out the big guns until the situation got dire, but her eyes filled with tears on their own.

"Please, guys?"

Her mother let out a long sigh. "Your father and I will talk about it again."

• • •

"'Talk about it again'?" Shelby Webber snapped as she followed Riley up the stairs that afternoon. "That's good, right?"

Riley gave her best friend a look.

"OK, it's not a definite no."

"Might as well be. How long does it take for them to talk about it? 'Hey, Ry should go on her school trip. Oh, OK.' Three seconds. Not an entire school day, which is like a lifetime in me-waiting-to-go-on-a-trip time."

Riley dumped her backpack on the floor and flopped down onto her bed. "Face it, Shelb. I'm trapped. I'm never going to get out of here. You'll go off to college, forget about me, and I'll be here, under curfew, reporting back to my parents."

Shelby's lips quirked up in a half smile. "Drama queen, party of one?"

"Shut up." Riley's stone gray eyes went up to Shelby, who was biting her lip, looking nervous. "What?"

"It's just—and I seriously hate to ask this, you know, because you're not going and all, but…"

Riley rolled her eyes. "Spit it out. What do you want?"

"Can I borrow your Hudson sweatshirt?"

"So you can ride up to Hudson without me, wearing my Hudson sweatshirt, *without* me?"

"Forget I said anything."

"No, no." Riley sighed as she pushed herself off the bed. "I'm going to die in this room anyway. Someone might as well get some use out of my clothes. The sweatshirt is probably still packed in one of the moving boxes." She jutted a thumb over her shoulder at the haphazard spread of torn-open cardboard boxes spread around the room.

"I can't believe you guys moved all the way out *here*." Shelby shuddered like the Blackwood Hills Estates, with its empty model homes and landscaping of mud and excess construction materials, was a hideous other planet. Which it kind of was.

"Thanks for coming all the way to outer Mongolia to visit me." Riley narrowed her eyes. "Unless it was all a ploy just to borrow my sweatshirt."

"I would never scam you that way, Ry. Not without getting some matching shoes or something too."

Riley poked through one of the boxes on her bedroom floor. "Oh, actually, it's probably in my parent's room."

Shelby followed Riley across the hall. "Why is it with their stuff?"

"Because technically, it's my dad's. It *was* my dad's. He got it when he was at Hudson. Never wears it anymore, so it's mine now."

"Whenever you sneak it out of their room."

Riley put her hands on her hips. "Do you want it or not?"

"Lead the way."

Riley put her hand on her parents' bedroom doorknob and turned to Shelby. "By the way, if anyone asks, we were never here. Ever."

Shelby looked around. "Your parents always let me come over."

"Not here, here! In my parents' room." Even as she said it, her heart skipped a little—but she smashed the niggling, rule-breaking guilt way down and piled her tethered-to-Crescent City annoyance on top of it. "We're not exactly supposed to be"—she made air quotes—"in there."

"Oh, Riley's breaking the rules!"

Riley narrowed her eyes and Shelby rolled hers. "Oh my God, Ry, your parents are, like, the nicest people on the planet. They're going to beat you if they find out you were in their room?"

"No! But they flip out over the weirdest things. When we were packing up the other house, I was trying to find some room for my shoes so I went through one of my dad's den boxes and he fully spazzed out."

"Awesome. We're going through the boxes of an unbalanced dude who can snap when people go through his boxes."

"He's not unbalanced. Just…wildly protective of office supplies?"

"Yep, that's logical."

Shelby let out a low whistle when Riley pushed her through the door to her parents' bedroom. "This is amazing. If you have to spend your whole life in the house anyway, you should have chosen this room."

"Would if I could. Here." Riley pushed open the closet and lugged out three enormous cardboard boxes. "It's in one of these. But other than the stuff in there, don't touch anything."

As if on cue, Riley's cell phone went off, a classic telephone ring that made her eyes roll. "It's like they know we're here." A hot stripe shot up the back of her neck, and she faked a cheerful voice. "Hi, Dad."

"Hey ya, turnip."

"Please, Dad—stop with the turnip stuff already."

"But you know how much I love turnips!"

Riley watched Shelby pacing the room, picking things up off her mother's dresser. She covered the phone and waved frantically at Shelby, mouthing, *don't touch anything!*

Shelby held her hands up and Riley had a fleeting thought that her father was just outside the bedroom door, ready to catch them both and sentence her to a lifetime grounding. She jumped when her father cleared his throat on his end of the phone.

"So, I guess you don't even want to know why I was calling."

Riley took a deep breath. "Hey, Dad, why are you calling?"

He chuckled. "Better. Anyway, your mother was here for lunch and we talked."

Riley held her breath, the edges of her stomach starting to quiver. "And?"

"And we've decided you can go on your school trip."

"Seriously?"

"Seriously."

Riley blinked, mouth open. Shelby just stared. "Wait," Riley said into the phone. "What's the catch?"

"There is no catch."

"There has to be. Like, you're chaperoning, or Mom slipped a GPS tracker into my Cheerios."

Her father chuckled again. "Nothing like that. But there are rules. We'll talk about them tonight over dinner."

"OK." Riley's grin was so big it hurt her cheeks. "Thanks, Dad."

Shelby rushed up to her, grabbing both wrists. "You're going. They're letting you go!"

"They're letting me go." Riley said the words slowly, and Shelby dropped her arms and stood back appraisingly.

"What is this that you're doing? This isn't the happy dance. This isn't the dance of 'we are spending an entire weekend on a college campus with no parents.' What dance is this?"

Riley's eyes swept her parents' room, the torn-open boxes. They had just given her permission to go on a trip even as she pawed through all their stuff…

She worried her bottom lip. "They're up to something."

"What are you talking about?"

"My parents never let me go anywhere. They never let me do anything. And suddenly, poof, they listen to me and let me go to another city? No."

"Maybe pod people ate your parents. Who cares? Your pod father gave you permission."

Riley looked up. "Maybe I shouldn't go."

Shelby slung her arm over Riley's shoulder and sat her gently on the bed. She dropped into a soothing voice as she petted Riley's hand. "What you're feeling is normal, Riley. There's even a name for it. It's called Stockholm syndrome."

Riley shoved Shelby but laughed. "Shut up!"

"You shut up. We're going away for the weekend! Be. Excited."

Riley thought about she and Shelby, lounging on a big green lawn in the shadow of a huge university and several university men.

"I'm excited."

After breaking into spontaneous happy dances and a short round of screams, Riley went back to the cardboard boxes. "OK, I feel kind of bad being in here, but now it's even more important. The sweatshirt for you and"—she disappeared waist-deep into one of the boxes and rifled around, coming up with a faded, vintage-looking Hudson tee—"this for me."

"We're going to be college girls!"

"No parents, free for the weekend!"

With gusto, Shelby dug into the box in front of her. Her flailing legs immediately stilled.

Riley stood. "Shelbs? Are you all right? Did a giant clothes rat eat your head off?"

"Oh my God!" Shelby flopped out of the box, cheeks red, maniacal grin spreading across her face. She waved a thick book with a pink gingham cover, the whole thing rimmed in eyelet lace. "Is this what I think it is?"

Riley crossed her arms in front of her chest, confused. "What do you think it is?"

Shelby climbed up on Riley's parents' bed and flopped on her stomach, chin in hands, book in front of her. Riley did the same.

"I think it's a tribute to the life of one cutesy-wutesy Wriley Spenca." She pinched one of Riley's cheeks. "Aww," she cooed, once she lifted the cover and revealed a wrinkled picture of Riley, dwarfed by a polka-dot-patterned baby blanket and a teeny little hat.

"I was a pretty cute baby," Riley said, grinning to herself.

"Nah, cute toddler. You were at least three in that pic."

"How do you know how old I was?"

"Are you kidding me? I can spot a toddler at eighty paces. And then I turn around and run the other way before my mom makes me babysit it."

Shelby went back to flipping through the pages while Riley hopped off the bed and continued shopping through her mother's clothes.

"Ugh. How do my parents expect any guy to look at me—let alone a college guy—in stuff like this?" Riley held up a particularly unflattering shirt with buttons in the shape of miniature horse heads.

Shelby just turned a page in the baby book, not bothering to look up. "A, that's probably their whole point and B, they probably expect you to wear your own clothes."

Riley groaned and dove back in the box where the album came from, grumbling about her mother's love of holiday turtlenecks.

"Ah ha!" she beamed a minute later, holding the Hudson sweatshirt up against her. She twirled, admiring herself in the mirror. "You know, now that I'm going on the trip too, maybe I should just wear this. It looks good on me, right?"

Shelby looked up. "Absolutely. You wear the sweatshirt I'm so totally borrowing, and I'll wear a sweatshirt with this on it." She held up the pink gingham album, open to a heinously embarrassing picture of four-year-old Riley on the toilet.

"You play dirty."

"You're the one on the toilet, toots. Sweatshirt, please."

Riley balled up the shirt and tossed it at Shelby, knocking the album right out of her hands and onto the floor.

"OK," Riley said, going back to the box. "We just need to get everything back in the box on Monday, and my parents will never notice."

Shelby picked up the album. "Um, they might notice you broke your baby book."

Anxiety pricked at the base of Riley's neck. Though her parents wouldn't let her go out for anything, they were pretty laid back when it came to just about anything else—as long as Riley followed the one cardinal rule: no going through their things.

Which inadvertently means no borrowing without asking, Riley thought. She immediately chased the thought away.

"It's just a couple of shirts," she muttered to herself.

"Hello?" Shelby said, holding up the book.

Riley snapped from her headspace. She crossed the room and took the baby book from Shelby, gingerly pulling at the paper that was now sticking out from the spine end.

"Oh," she said, relief crashing over her in waves. "It's not broken; there's just a little slit here in the cover. It's kind of hidden behind the bunny. See?" She held the book up for Shelby to inspect. "This was in there."

Shelby's eyes went wide. "What is it? Some kind of mysterious message?"

"Oh my God, Shelby, we need to find you a guy."

Riley pulled the paper out and unfolded it, sucking in a breath.

"What is it?"

Riley frowned. "Kind of a mysterious message. It's a birth certificate."

"Yours?"

Riley shook her head. "I don't think so."

TWO

Riley squinted at the birth certificate and turned it over and over in her hands. She had no idea why, but she studied every inch of it, certain that at some point there would be a "Made in China" or "Property of Disney" stamp. There was nothing.

"It looks authentic enough," Riley said with a frown. "I wonder who it belongs to."

Shelby grabbed the paper and scanned it. "It belongs to Jane Elizabeth O'Leary," she said. "O'Leary, that's Irish, right? Oh, me lucky charms! Maybe this kid was the leprechaun your parents stole for their pot of gold." She looked over the paper at Riley and raised her eyebrows.

"My parents don't have a pot of gold."

Shelby jutted her chin toward Riley's new attached bathroom. "Your own bathroom equals pot of gold in my book."

"You're so lame. So, Jane O'Leary, born May 14 to Seamus and Abigail O' Leary." Riley shook the paper in her hands. "Who are these people?"

"Ooh, baby Jane almost might have stolen your thunder. She

was born a whole thirteen months earlier. Maybe your mother had baby rage and had to do away with her."

Riley snorted. "We do know how violent my mother gets." She yanked an Easter turtleneck out of one of the boxes. "I mean just look at this. Bunnies. Easter eggs. Nadine Spencer is truly a madwoman." She tossed the turtleneck back but couldn't bring herself to toss the certificate.

Shelby gestured to it. "Are you going to ask your parents about your phantom sister? Tread lightly; they might knock you off next."

"I can't ask them about it. They would murder me—for real—if they knew I was in here, going through their stuff. I mean, the baby book wasn't exactly in plain sight." She chewed the inside of her cheek. "Seriously, who is this kid?"

"Hey, if you're that curious about ole Jane, Wiki that crap."

Riley carefully—but quickly—shoved everything but the baby book and her dad's sweatshirt back in the boxes and slid them back into place.

"Come on," she said, pulling Shelby by the hand.

They crossed the hall back into Riley's room. She yanked her laptop from under her bed and fired it up, tapping the baby's name into the Google search engine.

"OK, background check, background check, background check—only thirty-nine ninety-five. No on that one. Jane Elisabeth—Elisabeth with an *s*—is an ASU alum."

Shelby rooted through her backpack then stuck her arm into the Ruffles bag she yanked out. "She would be too old, unless our Jane is a genius. She's supposed to be only a year older than us."

"Then I'm assuming the obituary of eighty-nine-year old Jane Elizabeth O'Leary of Skokie, survived by her eleven adult children, is not our chick either." Riley chewed her bottom lip while she scanned page after page. "Our kid doesn't show up." She typed in the name of each of the parents separately and came up blank once more; it was the same when she tried the last name plus the name of the city, plus every other combination she could think of.

"According to Google, none of these people exist."

Shelby upturned the Ruffles bag and shook the last of the crumbs into her mouth. "Well, if you don't exist on Google, then you don't exist at all. Everyone knows that."

Shelby sat up with a start. "Ohmigod," she said, still chewing. "What if the birth certificate is actually yours? What if you're, like, one of the Amber Alerts? Or one of those *Have You Seen Me?* poster kids?" Her face was upturned, grease and salt from the chip bag glinting on the finger she used to point at Riley.

Riley rolled her eyes but got a little niggle of anxiety anyway. "That's stupid. This kid is a whole year older than I am."

"If they snatched you off the street, or out of some Walmart dressing room or something, they may have made you a year younger to throw people off the scent." Shelby narrowed her eyes suspiciously. "Is that your real hair color?"

Riley's hand flew to her head. She ran her hands through her pale, red-blond hair. "You know, you're right. I bet my mother comes in here every month and dyes my hair while I'm asleep!"

They were silent for a beat before Shelby's mouth dropped open again.

"OK, OK, how about this?" She started flapping her arms in an apparent attempt to take flight. "What if you're Amish, and your mom got knocked up on one of those Rumspringa hayrides? They weren't married, so once your mom had you, they were shunned, had to leave Amish-town, and then had to have a new birth certificate made for you! Because, you know, you were probably born in a barn or something."

She grinned, looking immensely pleased with herself, while Riley cocked an eyebrow. "So that's why we have that horse and buggy in the garage next to Mom's Mini Cooper!"

Shelby glared at Riley as if she were the one acting crazy. "Duh. They're ex-Amish. They would have adapted to our electronic American ways. No horse and buggy."

Riley let out an annoyed puff of air, and Shelby pointed at her. "I'm probably right, you know. You do have a ton of well-made wood furniture."

"Don't you have a boy band to stalk?"

"No, I'm between obsessions. OK, maybe you're not an Amish bastard. But it could be something else. Maybe one of your parents isn't actually your parent? Maybe one of your parents was married before and they had you. The marriage disintegrated amid rumors of abuse, but your mother couldn't prove it. You were supposed to go to your dad's for the summer, but she couldn't let that happen, so she went on the run with you. Your mom would have been on one of those underground railroads, and they made you a new birth certificate so your child-molester louse of a dad wouldn't find you. Think about it. You're an only child. You have no family, no cousins."

Riley waved the birth certificate. "Not me, Shelb." She pointed to the birth date again. "Not my birthday." Then the city of birth. "Granite Cay? Never been there. And this kid was—8.9 pounds! No way that's me." She tossed her hair over one shoulder and cocked out a hip. "I was a very svelte 6.1."

"I'm telling you, this is you. Have you ever seen your own birth certificate?"

"No."

Shelby bounded up, eyes wide. "Because there isn't one! I mean look, you and this Jane have the same eye color."

Riley's eyes widened. "Ohmigod. I didn't realize that. Blue-eyed girls are exceedingly rare."

Shelby's lips pressed into a hint of a smile but not enough to stop her from rambling on. "I bet if this kid had hair, it would be the same color as yours."

"You are being ridic."

"The milk carton kid all alone out here in suburbia where your real family could never track you down. No extended family to disprove my hypothesis…"

"That's because my parents were only children too. That's not that rare. Your mother was an only child."

"Which is why I am one of eight. My mom was so lonely as a kid she wanted to raise a basketball team when she grew up. Mission a-freaking-ccomplished."

"Big families aren't that weird, Shelbs."

Shelby made herself comfortable on Riley's mint-green comforter. "You have no idea how lucky you are."

For every silent moment at Riley's place, there was a crash, a shriek, or a stain at Shelby's. While Riley's parents needed to know—and approve—her every move from after-school activities to whether or not she ate enough breakfast, Shelby's parents did more of their parenting via headcount. If there were eight kids, everything was OK.

"Do you have anything else to eat?" Shelby asked, apparently already bored.

"You know the only way junk food gets in here is via the Shelbyville express." Riley glanced out her door. "I can probably smuggle you some kale chips or dark chocolate grasshoppers."

"See? Prison food. I'm telling you, Ry…" Her voice dropped to an ominous whisper. "Whatever happened to baby Jane? She's living in the suburbs and being force-fed kale chips!"

Riley considered for a second before flopping down on her bed next to Shelby, blinking up at the eggshell-white ceiling.

"So my parents snatched me off the street. How did they get my birth certificate then? And why did they keep it? Isn't that, like, evidence? The first thing you get rid of after committing a crime?"

Shelby's eyes sparkled as she inched toward Riley on the bed. "Maybe they stole you right from the hospital. Used to happen all the time. Or I guess you could have just been adopted." Shelby stuck out her tongue, obviously uninterested in the simplest solution.

"I wasn't adopted."

Shelby burst out laughing and tossed the birth certificate off the side of the bed. It floated down gently then Riley reached over to grab it.

"See? You can't quite let go…Jane."

"Shut up."

Shelby was silent for a beat then sighed dramatically. "I can't believe you. I can't believe you're not even the slightest bit curious."

Riley shrugged. "It's not that I'm not curious about it. I just—I don't know." She studied the certificate, scrutinizing it yet again. *Could there be something to this?* "My parents are my parents."

Shelby snatched the certificate back and raised her eyebrows. "Are they?"

Something shifted inside of Riley as she stared Shelby down. Shelby's brows were raised, her head cocked so that a shock of her dark hair snaked over her shoulder. Riley blinked. With her too-small, deep-set eyes, Shelby was a spitting image of her mother. They both had the same relaxed mouth, the same ski-jump nose that hooked just a smidge to the left.

"You're lame." Riley turned away from her friend, her eyes catching the picture she kept on her nightstand: Riley smashed between her mother and father, all three pressing their cheeks together. Riley had a big toothy grin with cheeks that were ruddy and round. Her father's smile was easy and relaxed, his narrow face regal next to Riley's. Her mother had high cheekbones and pale, porcelain skin, her heart-shaped lips pressed in a tight pink smile.

I don't look anything like them.

"What if your real parents are looking for you? Or what if they're, like, serial killers and that's why your adoptive parents, Glen and Nadine Spencer, are so hell-bent on hiding you from the outside world?" Shelby lowered her voice to a hoarse whisper. "They could have spies everywhere." She jabbed an index finger toward a construction worker leaning over the side of a cherry picker as he worked on a telephone cable outside. "He probably isn't even a telephone guy. He's probably sitting up there listening to everything we say."

"So is he spying for me or on me?" Riley was joking, trying to keep the conversation light, but she crossed the room and pulled the blinds anyway.

"You know I'm right. They've only let you spend the night at my house one time. One time!"

"Because I came home from that sleepover with gum in my hair."

"And how many other slumber parties have you gone to?"

Riley turned away. There was always a good excuse. Her father surprised her with a trip to Six Flags, so she had to skip Erica Fitzpatrick's twelfth birthday. And she was going to go to Cassie O'Hara's slumber party when she turned fourteen, but her mother got tickets to a musical in the city. She couldn't go to Shelby's last two slumber parties, but she couldn't exactly remember why.

Riley pushed the thoughts out of her head. Her parents weren't trying to hide anything…

She knew who she was. She knew who her parents were. But here was a birth certificate, hidden, buried away. Tangible proof that her parents didn't tell her everything.

"They probably pried you right out of your birth mother's arms."

"What are you talking about? My parents are the most polite—"

Shelby snatched a pillow off the bed and clutched it tight to her chest, pleading in a breathy Southern accent. "No, please, sir, not my baby! She's all I have!"

Riley wanted to say something back but couldn't form the words. Even as Shelby went on with her ridiculous rendition, Riley couldn't find the words to stop her.

"Oh my God. What if your dad had guns and he was all, 'pew! pew!' Like Wild Bill Hitchcock and stuff?"

"Hickok."

"What?"

"I'm pretty sure it was Wild Bill Hickok. And my dad doesn't have any guns." Riley made a conscious effort to stop biting her lower lip and whirled to face Shelby, who was pantomiming finger guns and kicking down doors. "Well, he has one gun, but it's like an antique or something. That's not weird though, right?"

"Not according to the NRA."

"Does your dad have any?"

Shelby looked over the top of the magazine she had just picked up. "Are you kidding? Eight kids? My parents are unfortunately all about the making love, not war." She shuddered.

Riley swallowed and tried to force a smile at Shelby's joke. But her mind was already spinning off in a thousand different directions. What if…

"No, you're being stupid and you're making me paranoid. This thing probably just came with the baby book, and my parents are overprotective just because they are, and my dad has a super old-fashioned gun that his dad gave him or something."

Shelby flipped a page in her magazine. "Whatever makes you feel better, Ry."

"That's not weird." Riley spoke defiantly to Shelby's bent head and the couple on the cover of *US* magazine—but she wasn't sure who she was trying to convince.

"Of course not, Ry. It's like in the Constitution or the habeas corpus or whatever. Americans can have guns and parents can be paranoid. No big."

Riley sat delicately at the end of her bed, and Shelby put down her magazine and straightened.

"Are you seriously freaked out about this?"

"No—no, it's just, I don't know—"

"A coincidence?"

Riley turned to face her friend. "Coincidence? Five seconds ago, my dad was a baby-stealing Wild Bill Hickok."

"I'm pretty sure it's Hitchcock. And why don't you just ask to see your real birth certificate or something? If they won't let you, then you know." Shelby's eyes were glazing again as she came up with a new storyline for Riley's so-called life. "And then you can confront them with the evidence."

"And what am I supposed to say? 'Hey, Mom, Dad, did you snatch me away from my birth parents?'"

Now Shelby was biting her bottom lip. "Right. If they really are criminals, accusing them like that could make them snap. That could be their trigger."

"Their trigger?"

"For going on a murderous rampage. And since you have no next-door neighbor, I would have to give the interview saying that the Spencers were nice, quiet people who kept to them-selves mostly. The girl seemed well adjusted, nice enough. Kind of paranoid, but I guess that's to be expected of a child cut out of her own mother's womb."

Riley crossed her arms in front of her chest. "So now my parents aren't just kidnappers; they're psychopaths on a murderous rampage who cut me out of my mother's womb."

"It's possible I watch too much TV."

• • •

Shelby blew Riley a kiss before dancing down the newly constructed front steps and locking herself in her Toyota Corolla—a rusting, paint-chipped heap that lacked a left turn signal but had a radio that could be heard from space. She cranked up a Death to Sea Monkeys song, and Riley poked her head in through the passenger side window while she and Shelby belted out the last refrain of "Underwater Universe." At the last drumbeat, Riley stepped away, watching the Corolla roll down the driveway and into the street.

Riley suddenly felt very alone—last person in the world alone—as she watched Shelby's ancient clunker head away from the house. The car looked remarkably out of place against the stark, modern houses all lined up in orderly rows. She stood on the porch, watching as the sun dipped, bleeding a heavy pink into the twilight. There was no sound out here. No sirens, no cars, no horns or echoed conversation, and suddenly the birth certificate, the emptiness, struck an icy finger of fear down the back of Riley's neck.

I'm being ridiculous.

But still she couldn't tear her eyes from scanning the horizon, from scrutinizing every house she could see: the black, gaping windows, empty driveways, open roads. It looked as if she was in a universe all her own, as if someone had sucked up every human being and left everything else as it was. Out here, all alone, in the middle of nowhere.

Riley thought of the birth certificate, of Shelby's ridiculous stories about Riley being snatched and hidden away from her "real" family.

But if you wanted to keep something hidden, the Blackwood Hills Estates was the place to do it.

Riley's phone was chirping with a missed text when she came back into the house.

RY-PIE DAD & I ARE GOING TO BE LATE. 9:30? EAT SOMETHING. DO HOMEWORK. LV MOM

She instinctively called back, chewing the inside of her cheek while her mother's phone rang and rang.

Did they ever say where they were going?

Random, irrational scenarios played out in Riley's head: her parents were shopping for another child. They were spying on her birth parents. They were going to check on Jane.

She shook her head and laughed at herself for letting Shelby's crazy ideas get to her. Her parents were her parents, and they were late because they were at a fundraiser or at her father's work or watching one of their mega-boring foreign films.

But baby Jane…

Riley shimmied the birth certificate out from the biology

textbook she had absently shoved it in and settled herself in front of her laptop. She typed JANE ELIZABETH O'LEARY into the search engine, culling through the pages and pages of hits that came up. When she exhausted her Google search, she tried out a few others—People Search, People Find, Yellow Pages. Each turned up a handful of names that semi-matched her search parameters, but nothing was a direct match. Riley snatched up the birth certificate then carefully typed in Jane's city and state of birth, Granite Cay, Oregon. The same pages she had filtered through the night before popped up, but this time, a little animated map also showed up as well. Riley clicked on it then felt her breath catch. Granite Cay, Oregon, was just a few inches from the California university she was about to visit.

When the doorbell rang, she sat bolt upright, not immediately recognizing the slow, melodic chimes.

No one had ever come to visit yet.

Heart thumping from the start, she picked her way down the stairs carefully, turning on lights as she went, each splashing a wash of yellow over the few family pictures that lined the walls.

"Who is it?" she called as she reached the door.

No one answered.

Riley paused, half crouched, her hand on the doorknob. She breathed hard before rolling up on her toes and squinting through the peephole.

There could have been someone there, but Riley couldn't tell through the blackness. She couldn't remember if the porch light had a bulb yet.

Had someone taken it? Had it ever been there to begin with?

Her heart started to pound, her mind throbbing, clogging with images: a police officer, come to take her away; Seamus and Abigail O'Leary, wringing their hands while looking for their daughter Jane; a lackey for her parents, certain they knew what Riley had found.

Stop being a paranoid freak, she commanded herself.

She was breathing hard now, her runaway mind pretzeling her body into a panic attack. She felt the telltale beads of sweat on her upper lip and at her hairline. Her chest felt as if it had been wrapped tight, every breath she tried to take an exhausting effort.

"I'm OK, I'm OK." She spat out the mantra Dr. Morley had told her to say, and concentrating on the words did calm her, slowly, each syllable carefully chipping away at the block that held down Riley's lungs. She paced the front room, peeking out the long window there to see that there was no one on the porch, no one parked on the streets.

A glitch, Riley decided. The bell had rung due to a mechanical glitch.

When she was breathing normally again, deep breaths in, long breaths out, she double-checked the lock on the door. It was locked. Riley had initially liked the thick, heavy bolt on the door, but that little niggling voice in the back of her head was suddenly wondering whether it was there to keep the bad people out—or in.

Back upstairs, Riley shoved the birth certificate aside and yanked her biology book closer. She was done being Nancy Drew—an errant doorbell had nearly made her pee her pants—but it was what was on her computer screen that caused the blood in her veins to run ice-water cold.

The headline letters were thick, an almost throbbing red. **HAVE YOU SEEN ME?** The picture underneath was a grainy black and white of a chubby, round-cheeked baby girl. There was no name, no contact number, no additional information.

"Oh my God," Riley breathed. "My God."

Riley didn't recognize the baby—nothing about her seemed familiar—but her black eyes were round and wide.

Trusting.

My sister?

She found herself leaning in and pulling the laptop closer as she scrutinized the screen. Did this baby have her eyes, a lopsided smile like her own?

Her stomach started to churn, bile burning at the back of her throat.

Or is that me? The phrase zipped through Riley's head, was gone before she had a chance to catch it.

She shoved the computer from her as though it were a snake, coiled and ready to bite. But it wasn't the child or the missing poster that scared her the most—it was how the webpage ended up on her screen.

With trembling fingers, she pulled down her web browser history, alternately praying for some easy explanation or for the photo to disappear—or to never have existed at all. The history popped up as quickly as it faded out when the screen went black.

The lights zapped out.

Riley went to the window. Her heart was beating in her throat, pounding in her ears, the sound like thundering footsteps. Her whole body was humming with adrenaline electricity, but all of that stopped when she saw the figure in the front seat of the dark car parked in front of her driveway. Her breath was choked, strangling. She wanted to pound the window, she wanted to scream, but her voice was lost in the gunning engine of the car. Her cry was muffled by the pinching squeal of tires speeding off into the darkness.

• • •

Riley didn't remember falling asleep.

She remembered being curled into a tight, uncomfortable ball underneath her bedroom window, the sound of those tires ricocheting through her skull until she couldn't take it anymore. Every muscle in her body was tense and exhausted from hours on high alert. After the picture on the computer screen and the realization that someone might have been watching her, Riley waited, unmoving, for the lights to come back on in the house. She waited for her parents to come home. Somewhere between those two, she must have pulled herself into bed and fallen into an achingly deep sleep.

She dreamed of Jane Elizabeth O'Leary—a naked, chubby-faced baby girl with Riley's features and Riley's grin. In her dream, she was at the beach and baby Jane was sitting in the sand in front of her, the tide coming in and washing over her fat baby thighs. Baby Jane squealed and slapped at the shallow water, looking up at Riley as it receded. Riley felt herself grin until she saw the next wave coming in. It crashed a little later than the first one did, and the tide swallowed Jane's thighs and came up to her chest, receding much more slowly this time. Another wave smacked the shore, and Riley knew that it would lift the baby from the sand and suck her backward out to sea. She couldn't let that happen. Riley ran toward Jane as the water made its way in, but the sand was wet and heavy underneath her feet. She tried to warn Jane, but it was as if the sand had moved into her throat, snatching her breath, her voice. She sank deeper and deeper into the wet sand as the water snaked around Jane, narrow fingers snatching at her. Riley clawed at the ground, trying to move as the water whooshed over Jane's head, slapping against the sand, teasing the tips of Riley's fingers. When the water receded, Jane was gone.

Riley couldn't get the dream out of her mind. Who *was* Jane? Was Jane missing, out in the world, alone somewhere? Or was Riley really Jane? Could there be some truth to Shelby's crazy stories?

Stolen. Riley could have been stolen; she could have been kidnapped.

"No," she said to herself as she stepped into the shower. "I was not kidnapped. My parents aren't criminals."

Adopted?

The word shot through Riley's mind, and she fought to press it down.

"You're being ridiculous. Your parents are your parents. I was not kidnapped." She repeated the words so many times they lost meaning, and the niggling feeling was back at the fringe of her mind, tapping: *but what if?*

She dressed quickly, finding herself validating her every move: *the blue shirt. Her favorite color. Was it her favorite color? Her mother bought it for her. She remembered the wry grin as she handed it over and Riley—naïve, innocent Riley—held it to her chest.*

"It's blue—your favorite. I couldn't resist."

Riley narrowed her eyes. "Why? Are you trying to butter me up or something?"

"Can't a mother pick up a shirt for her daughter?"

Her mother grinned then, a smile Riley once thought was a larger version of her own. But it wasn't really. Her mother's lips were pouty and full with a constant deep pink hue. Riley's were pin thin and she was eternally painting them with Cool Coral lip gloss just so they would show up.

"Ry? Are you coming down? You're going to be late!"

Riley stepped carefully down the stairs as if each one was a minefield—was she a missing child, stolen, or wasn't she? She paused to study the few family pictures on the wall—her smiling as a toothless second grader, the family at the beach the year they lived near Carmel. Why had they moved again?

"Riley Allen Spencer, I'm not going to ask you again."

"Sorry!" Riley said, entering the kitchen as she had done a thousand mornings before. Her parents were looking at her, and heat shot up the back of her neck. *Did they know what she found? Did they know what she suspected?*

"What's up, guys?" she asked, doing her best to act nonchalant.

"We could ask you the same thing," her father said, eyes dropping back to his paper.

Riley snapped bolt upright. "What's that supposed to mean?"

"It means," her mother said as she pulled out Riley's chair, "that we don't usually have to send in the brigade to get you out of bed."

Riley felt her cheeks redden. "I guess I just overslept."

"Well, eat up. You're not going to school on an empty stomach. And you have the carnival tonight too, right?"

Her father looked up, eyes bright. "A carnival?"

"It's a dumb school thing. Fund-raiser."

"Eat."

Riley reached for the cereal box and looked down at her bowl before she poured. It was the china she had remembered since—*when?* The napkin, the spoon, the juice glass—and the little white pill.

Every morning, Riley's mother set the breakfast table, and every morning it looked this same way: cereal bowl, napkin, spoon, juice glass, little white pill. It was Klonopin, an antianxiety medication that the therapist back in Riley's old neighborhood—where she lived next door to Shelby—had prescribed. It helped Riley focus, staved off her fears, and was supposed to keep the nightmares at bay. Every day, her mother set out the pill, and every day, Riley swallowed it. Every month, her mother refilled her prescription, and every month, Riley never questioned the white plastic bottle that her mother stashed in the medicine cabinet.

"Don't forget your pill, hon."

Riley's stomach fluttered madly. This was crazy. This was *her mother.* The tiny white pill blurred and swam in front of Riley's eyes. *What if the doctor was in on it? What if this wasn't even the pill he prescribed?*

She scrutinized the thing, hoping that etched there across the face would be something to put her mind at ease: RILEY'S KLONOPIN FOR ANXIETY or NOT SOME SORT OF KNOCK-OUT DRUG.

"I'm no doctor, turnip, but I'm pretty sure the pill works best when you actually put it in your mouth and swallow it."

Her father was smiling kindly, his glasses dipping down his nose as he eyed Riley.

"What if I don't want to take it?"

Riley's mouth was dry, and her pulse was pounding in her ears. How would they react?

"Well, if you don't think you need to take them anymore, we can go see Dr. Morley."

"Why do I need to see the doctor to stop taking them?"

"Because it could be dangerous, Ry. That's why I give them to you every morning, you nut. If you skip doses, you can get a stomachache, your panic attacks could come back, or worse."

Riley swung her head toward her mother. "What do you mean worse?"

"You'll grow chest hair." Her father folded the paper. "Now swallow that pill and that bowl of whats-it-snaps and let's get in the car. You're going to make me late for work."

Riley popped the pill into her mouth and took a big gulp of juice, the bitter liquid burning her throat. She grabbed her backpack, and when her father leaned in to kiss her mother, Riley spat the slimy pill into her hand and tucked it into her jeans.

• • •

"The bus is leaving," Riley's father said, slamming the car door hard. The reverberation echoed through the quiet neighborhood. Riley was halfway into the passenger seat before she slapped her forehead.

"Crap. Forgot my purse."

She pushed herself out of the car but was unable to escape her mother's narrowed eyes as she stood in the doorway. "Sorry, Mom," Riley mumbled as she jogged past her into the house.

Riley's hand was on the knob when a movement at the house across the street caught her eye. Riley squinted hard, trying to focus, but the glare of the sun bouncing off the glass hurt her eyes. She was only able to make out a shadowy silhouette—a person or a bundle of leftover construction stuff?

My God, Ry, you're really going crazy now. Criminal parents, spies in empty houses…I'm going to kill Shelby when I get to school.

"Come on, Ry!" her father said.

Riley bounded into the car and belted herself in. As they backed down the driveway, she glanced up at the house again, but now there was nothing in the window.

"So, did someone move into the house across the street?"

"No," her father said. "I don't think it's ready yet. I talked to one of the realtors last week, and she said the workers had broken a back window. Which reminds me—I promised your mother we'd go over the rules for your trip."

Riley groaned. "I know Mom's rules. Don't talk to strangers, don't take anything from strangers, never leave my Coke unattended. Stop, drop, and roll." She grinned at the last one.

"Mom and I just don't want you to forget. You were asleep by the time we got home last night, and you left the front door unlocked. A good gust of wind would have blown it wide open."

THREE

Ice water shot through Riley's veins, paralyzing every inch of her.

I locked the door, she wanted to shout. *I know I did.*

She bit her lower lip to hold back tears. Her dad must have seen her expression, because he leaned over and patted her thigh. "Don't worry, hon. We're not mad at you. It happens. Just make sure you don't let it happen again." His words sounded hollow though.

Riley nodded, clenching her jaw. She blinked, and the missing poster flashed behind her eyelids, those wide, dark eyes of the little girl burning into her soul.

"D-d-dad," she started. Then, steeling herself, "Dad, there was some—"

What little voice she had was cut off by the shrill ring of her father's phone. He held up a single finger to Riley and pressed the answer button on his earpiece.

"Glen Spencer." He cocked his head for a microsecond while Riley tried to gather her thoughts and then start again. *Sorry,* he mouthed, *client.*

They made the rest of the drive in silence.

By three o'clock, Riley and Shelby had dumped their backpacks in Shelby's trunk and were stuffing french fries in their mouth as they watched carnies snapping together rides in the back forty.

"I can't believe we have to spend our whole night volunteering at this stupid thing. Don't they know I have to pack?"

"Shelbs, we're going to be gone for one night. How hard is it to pack for that?"

"It's one night on a college campus. And why are you so gung ho on the carnival?" She pointed a fry at Riley. "Wait. Are you all into the carnival, or is your alter ego, Jane O'Leary, all into it?"

Riley rolled her eyes. "Neither of us are really into clowns and carnies, but both of us are into getting volunteer hours."

"So you admit it! You're one of those kids on a missing poster!"

Riley rolled her eyes. "You know what? I can't wait until you get a concussion in the dunking booth. Anything to make you stop talking about the birth certificate. You have me freaking out and thinking horrible things about my parents."

"They have done horrible things." She made the universal face for "gag." "Like buying rice chips and seaweed."

Riley wiped her palms on her jeans and straightened her green and white Hawthorne Hornets bow. "Are you ready to go?"

Shelby leveled the giant hornet head over her own. "I really can't believe they let you run the change booth and they made me the stupid hornet."

"Hey!" Riley frowned. "Henry the Hornet is a beloved mascot. And if you didn't fail math this year, Mr. Rose would trust you to count money. Your stinger is sagging, by the way."

Shelby grunted inside the giant, fabric-covered hornet head. "Just for that, I'm sending all the creepy clowns to your booth."

Riley spent the evening making change and nursing a large Coke. Shelby hadn't made good on her promise, but Riley kept an eye on her anyway, catching Henry's giant hornet head as Shelby waddled through the crowd, her antennae bobbing with each step. The crowds were starting to die down, and Riley yawned then waved across the midway to where Shelby was hiding out—a little shadowed *V* underneath the Tilt-A-Whirl.

Riley beckoned her over.

"I can't believe you're still in that ridiculous costume. I thought you would have ditched it hours ago."

Henry the Hornet shrugged.

"Can you watch my booth? I've had to pee since we walked in." Riley edged her way out of the booth and beelined through the crowd, not waiting for Shelby to answer. She was halfway back when Shelby—sans Henry costume—sidled up next to her.

"Hey! Who's watching my booth?"

Shelby shrugged. "I give up. Who's watching your booth?"

"It's not a joke; it's a question. You were supposed to be watching it."

Shelby's eyebrows rose. "Did you find one of those vodka Slurpees?"

"Shelbs, I'm serious! How did you get out of your Henry costume so fast?"

"I've been out of that thing for hours. Paid Trevor Gallagher ten bucks to take over."

Heat snaked up Riley's spine. She pointed. "Trevor Gallagher is right there."

"No, he's—who the hell is wearing the Henry costume?"

Henry's big head bobbed up and cocked, his enormous bug eyes seeming to pin Riley back. He raised a hand and waved then turned on his heel and disappeared behind a bank of food carts.

Riley yanked her purse out from under the booth and searched through it then pulled out the cash box. "It doesn't look like he took anything."

"But who the hell was that? Hey, Trevor!" Shelby yelled.

Trevor trotted over, giving a short nod to Riley.

Shelby put her hands on her hips. "You were paid good money to be Henry. He's a beloved mascot!"

Trevor shrugged. "You paid me ten bucks to be Henry for an hour."

"Then who is Henry right now?"

"I don't know. I took that thing off the minute the hour was up. That head smells like ass. I should have asked for fifty bucks."

"Well, where did you put it after you took it off?" Riley asked.

"Back in the band box. Geez, lay off." Trevor turned away, disappearing back into the crowd.

Riley found Henry again.

"There he is. Stay here." Riley jogged across the fairway, poking her head behind the food carts. She saw Henry's giant antennae snaking around a taco truck. "Hey!" She followed him around the corner, but it was only Henry's head, settled over the folded hornet costume.

"So?" Shelby jogged up behind her, Riley's purse slung over her shoulder, the change in the cash box rattling as she ran.

Riley shrugged. "I don't know. Whoever it was changed and left the costume right here."

"OK, so we have a random person who likes to run around in a stolen hornet costume. That is gross on so many levels."

She handed Riley her purse and the cash box and gathered up the Henry costume.

"I have to go turn this back in. Turn in the cashbox and meet me at the car, OK?"

Riley nodded, even as unease pricked out all over her. She grabbed the back of Shelby's shirt and followed her out of the food truck shadows and onto the well-lit fairway.

"I just got the chills."

"I'm thinking someone in a stolen hornet costume will do that to you," Shelby said with a grin.

Riley dropped off the cashbox and was waiting at Shelby's car, tapping her foot. "Where the hell are you, Shelby?"

She rooted around in her purse, looking for her cell phone. When she pulled it out, there was a postcard half sticking out of the case.

Riley frowned. It was a black-and-white photo of some kids—teenagers, mostly—dressed in funky 1970s clothing. They were all slouching in front of a brick wall, a fading four-leaf clover painted just above their heads.

"Love note?" Shelby asked as she came up over Riley's shoulder.

"No, I just found it in my purse." She turned the postcard over and read the note:

"*Something lost has now been found.* And there's a red circle around the word *found.*"

"Um, OK. In terms of love notes, I've read better. Who's it from?"

"I have no idea." Riley waved the card. "There's no signature, and I don't recognize the writing."

"And it was in your purse?"

"Yeah, that's so weird."

"Not if it's from your birth parents." Shelby waggled her eyebrows. "Or maybe it's from Jane O'Leary, trying to contact you from beyond the grave." She did her best impression of spooky fingers and ghost voice, but Riley was not amused.

"You really need to stick to your stories, Shelbs. Am I the missing kid, or is the missing kid my knocked-off big sister?"

Shelby gunned the engine. "I don't know. You're the one getting ghost posts."

• • •

Shelby pulled the car into Riley's driveway and pushed it into park. "So tomorrow morning, bright and early?"

"Definitely. I can't wait." Riley slammed the door shut, and Shelby rolled down the window, grunting with the effort of cranking the handle.

"Don't let the fake hornet get you. Oh! I bet it was your birth mother, closing in on you! She's sending you mystery postcards to warn you…"

"Shelby! If I were adopted, my parents wouldn't have changed my age and my birth date. Stop with this!"

"But if your—"

"Drive away, Shelby."

Shelby rolled down the street, giggling, as Riley headed for the front door. She paused when her hackles went up, her whole body stiff with the sudden fear that she was being watched. She spun slowly, squinting at the vacant houses that lined the street around her. When nothing jumped out, she let out a long sigh.

She tried to brush the feeling off but it stuck; she sped up the walk and locked the door behind her.

"How was the carnival, turnip?"

Riley jumped when her father came down the hall. "Creepy."

Her father looked alarmed. "Did someone bother you?"

She thought briefly of telling her dad about the fake Henry or the weird postcard, but she knew it would only lead to two things: her parents' insane overreaction and her parents' insane overprotection. They would call the police, and Riley would never be able to leave the house again, let alone go on the school trip.

"It was nothing. Just some stupid kids or something." Riley paused. Maybe it was the strangeness of the night or a sudden boldness at being allowed to spend the weekend away, but she asked, "Did you and Mom ever want another kid?"

Her father paused then sat down on the stairs, patting the space next to him for Riley to sit. She did.

"Is this because you didn't win a goldfish?"

"What—no!"

"Honey, I know how hard those carnival games can be. If you really want a goldfish, Mom and I will get you one. It'll be a lot faster than making you a baby sister."

Riley rolled her eyes when her father laughed.

"I was being serious, Dad."

He swung an arm over Riley's shoulder. "Why would we want another kid when we've got perfection right here? We hit pay dirt the first time around." He gave her a loud, smacking kiss on the forehead then patted the top of her head and shuffled up the stairs. Riley didn't move from her spot even when he turned off the hallway light, leaving only the faint upstairs glow bleeding in the hallway.

Was it weird that he immediately mentioned a sister? Riley thought absently.

• • •

Shelby was standing in front of the school the next morning, checking her phone and glancing up occasionally. She broke into a wide grin as Riley waved good-bye to her parents. "I. Am. So. Excited." She was talking in fully punctuated sentence-words and flapping her arms—Shelby always did when she got excited. Riley grabbed her friend and brushed down her arm-wings.

"Calm down, Shelbs. You're about to take flight."

But Riley didn't quite feel as cool as she acted. She looked around, little goose bumps rising on the back of her neck. She always found being on campus eerie when classes weren't going on—even more so on a Saturday morning like this. It almost seemed like school should cease to exist between Friday night and Monday morning.

"Hey!" Shelby calmed down and pinched Riley. "I called you, like, three times last night. No answer. What'd you do?"

"Nothing. Ate pizza, ran a few more Google searches."

"Oh, on your parent-felons?"

"My parents aren't felons!" Riley hissed. "Besides, it didn't turn up anything, felons or not."

"Did I hear someone mention felons?"

As if Jonathan "JD" Davison's voice wasn't distinctive enough—it was deeper and smoother than any other high school guy Riley had ever encountered—the fact that he showed up once the word "felon" was mentioned was all kinds of indication.

JD was the kid every parent hoped didn't hang out with theirs—and Riley's parents topped that list. He had been dubbed JD—for juvenile delinquent—from his numerous stints in the principal's office and his not-so-private run-ins with the Crescent City Police Department. Normally a guy like JD wouldn't cross into a world like Riley's—accelerated classes, the "good" kids on college tracks—but Riley's new, longer trek to Hawthorne High paired with her love for sleep landed them smack dab in the same detention period for a week straight almost a month ago. She had pushed the "I overslept" envelope, and he was warming his usual spot.

She remembered the scrutinizing way he looked at her when she walked into the empty classroom.

"You're new," he muttered.

Riley gripped the straps of her shoulder bag and slipped into the desk furthest away from JD. She was horrified to be in detention and not exactly eager to make friends with someone who always seemed to be in trouble for something. Her parents were going to freak out enough already.

JD turned in his seat, his dark eyes following her every move. "What are you in for?"

She pulled her knees up to her chest. "Tardies. You?"

"Truancy, gambling on campus, just being my charming self."

Riley cocked an eyebrow. "Oooh, you're a regular James Dean rebel."

JD looked impressed. "You know James Dean?"

Riley crossed her arms in front of her chest. "Why is that such a surprise?"

"I don't know. I figured your vintage would be Johnny Depp, pre-Jack Sparrow."

Riley feigned confusion. "Johnny who now?"

JD laughed, and her wall of ice was beginning to melt. "My parents and I like to watch old movies," she said. "We pop a bunch of popcorn, grab a couple of Cokes, and watch till our eyes cross—or until my dad starts with his impressions. He does a mean Jimmy Stewart."

"Really?"

"No, it's awful."

Riley and JD spent the next week whispering until the detention monitor glared or threatened them. She liked his wild streak, his care-lessness. On the last day, he waved to her.

"See you, Spence."

"You act like we're never going to see each other again."

He shrugged. "We both know how this works."

Riley watched him disappear into a sea of black leather and spiky hair. She turned, linking arms with her own friends—preppy shirts, Hawthorne High ribbons, and straight As.

"Ugh, JD," Shelby whispered.

"Back off, Shel. He's actually kind of cool."

Shelby crossed her arms in front of her chest and cocked out one hip, her eyes zeroing in on JD. "They have you doing detention here on Saturdays now too?"

"Actually, I'm here for the tour," JD replied.

"Cool," Riley said.

Shelby gaped next to her. "Seriously?"

Riley felt color wash her cheeks. She glanced up, but JD was unaffected. "Always nice to chat with you, Shelby. Ry." He gave her a curt nod then turned on his heel. Riley watched him go, thinking that from the back, he looked way less felon, way more runway model.

"Earth to Ry!" Shelby started snapping her fingers a millimeter from Riley's nose. "We're getting on the bus."

Riley stumbled out of her reverie and hiked her backpack up. Shelby laced an arm through hers and dragged her toward the bus.

"So you know what? I've decided to use this opportunity to break out of my shell. I'm going to make friends. I'm going to talk to boys."

"My little Shelby Webber? Talk to boys?"

Riley could see the fear wash over Shelby's face. "OK, maybe I should pretend to be a foreign exchange student on this trip. You know, practice as someone else before I break out the Shelby."

Riley cocked a brow. "From what country? You've had three years of Spanish and still can only ask for two Cokes or how much that sombrero is."

Riley glanced over her shoulder when she heard JD's low laugh. He followed them on the bus, taking a seat across from them as they got situated in the back.

"So, JD, are you taking any of the classes on the tour?" Riley asked casually.

JD's eyes flicked over Riley's. "Nah. I got in to Berkeley."

Shelby launched herself across the bus seat and over Riley's lap. "*You're* going to Berkeley? Like the school?"

JD nodded, his eyes still on Riley. "Yeah. Early admissions." He narrowed his eyes at her, and Riley felt herself flush.

"What?"

He shrugged. "I don't know. You just don't seem like the Hudson type."

Riley's eyebrows rose. "The Hudson type?"

"Preppy. Boring."

Shelby leaned over Riley a second time. "I'll have you know that Riley's dad is a preppy, boring Hudson alum."

"Undergrad," Riley clarified.

Shelby waggled her eyebrows as she yanked her tablet from her purse. "Your dad is borderline hot now, Ry. I bet he was smokin' in college."

"That's disgusting on so many levels, Shelbs."

Shelby ignored her, swiping until the Hudson University Alumni Association home page popped up.

"So, JD, if you already got into Berkeley, what are you doing on this trip?" Riley asked.

JD kicked his boots up on the empty bus seat next to him and knotted his hands behind his head. "Let's just say this bus will get me where I need to go."

Riley snaked her arms in front of her chest. "What's that supposed to mean?"

Shelby broke away from her tablet. "He's probably planning

a bank heist. Hey! Maybe he can help you with your new life of crime!"

JD's eyebrows went up, disappearing into a shock of his dark hair. "Sweet little Riley Spencer is engulfed in a life of crime? What an interesting development."

"It's nothing," Riley said, glaring at Shelby.

Shelby went back to her tablet, wrinkling her nose and frowning. "Did your dad take your mother's last name by any chance?"

"Of course not. So, JD—"

Shelby nudged her. "I'm serious, Ry."

Riley straightened. "What are you talking about?"

Shelby sucked in a deep breath and turned the tablet to face Riley. "Because according to the alumni association, the student registry, and the yearbook, Glen Spencer never existed at Hudson."

"You probably spelled his name wrong. Or got the dates wrong. His class probably isn't even online anyway."

"It goes all the way back to class of 1980."

Riley took the tablet and began a new search. "Why would my dad lie about being an undergrad at a stupid university?"

"Right," JD laughed from his seat. "If I was going to lie about school, I'd tell everyone I went to Harvard or Oxford."

Shelby cocked an eyebrow. "Or Berkeley?"

"What's your problem, Shelby?"

Riley heard JD snapping and Shelby quipping back, but she couldn't concentrate on the words. Her fingers were moving, constantly typing and retyping her father's name until the string of letters looked like gobbledygook before her eyes. But the search result was always the same: *Your search for* Glen Morgan Spencer *yielded 0 results.*

She handed Shelby the tablet, unease settling in her gut. Shelby's eyes were soft, questioning, and Riley shrugged, feeling the need to explain.

"It's nothing," she said. "Probably just a mix-up at the registrar's office or something."

"Yeah, totally." Shelby nodded emphatically and slid the tablet into her bag, popping in her ear buds instead.

Riley glanced around the dimly lit bus as her classmates' voices started to fade. Kids started to settle in, the rhythmic whir of the engine lulling most to sleep, but Riley's eyes were wide open, her thoughts buzzing like hornets in her mind.

My dad wasn't at Hudson?

"Hey," JD said, pulling Riley out of her thoughts. "So you're planning on going to Hudson, then?"

Riley paused, biting the inside of her cheek. "Where is the bus taking you?"

"Um, OK." JD leaned forward and dropped his voice. "I'm going to take the train to Rosemont." He flipped his iPad around so the screen faced Riley. "Going to see my favorite band."

"Oh my God! That's right! You love Death to Sea Monkeys too! How far is Rosemont?"

"It's a forty-minute train ride from Boone."

Out of nowhere, a thought popped into Riley's head. Rosemont was a forty-minute ride from Boone. Boone was a two-hour ride to the California-Oregon border.

And Granite Cay, Jane Elizabeth O'Leary's birth town, was just across that border.

Suddenly, Riley's palms itched. The birth certificate burned in her bag where she—on a whim—had stashed it.

That morning, Riley piled her bag with vintage tees and her usual cache of jeans, a Mom-approved stash of in-case-of-hospital clean underwear and bras, and, for some reason, the birth certificate. She had sat at her desk and rubbed her finger over the onion-skin sheet, over the names typed in more than a decade ago. *Who was baby Jane Elizabeth and where was she now?* The question pulled at her. She had traced her tiny footprints and handprints and felt a weird sense of longing, of connection to the baby—and the baby's parents—who had come into her world, floating around like balloons without strings.

Riley looked from Shelby—who had her ear buds in and was bopping in her seat—to JD. *Sometimes I feel like I have no connection, no root, nothing tying me to my life, to my brand-new bedroom in our brand-new tract home—to anything,* Riley thought. She felt as disconnected and as forgotten as baby Jane, tucked away in a baby book somewhere, dumped in a box, forgotten until unearthed by accident. Tears stung at the back of her eyes.

"So what do you do? You can't just walk out." She jutted her head toward the front of the bus where Ms. Carter sat, her profile lit by the greyish light of her iPad. "Carter counts."

"Or miscounts."

"What's that supposed to mean?" she asked.

"If you're not here for the first head count, she's not going to be missing you for the one later. She doesn't look like a teacher who's lost students, and we get a couple of extra hours to really explore. Why? You gonna come with me?"

Riley glanced out the bus window, her mother's admonitions ringing through her head. She could get lost or murdered or kidnapped—

Her stomach turned to liquid.

What if she already *had* been kidnapped?

Riley turned back to JD. "So how do you make Carter mess up her count?"

• • •

Riley's heart sped up as the bus slowed down. Shelby's head was lolled to the side, her temple against Riley's shoulder, her lips slightly parted as she snored. Riley glanced down at her then gave her a small shake.

"Shelby!"

"What?"

Riley bit her bottom lip. She never lied to Shelby, never kept anything from her. "I'm not going to go on the tour."

Shelby gaped. "What are you talking about?"

"Jane."

Shelby rolled her eyes. "What about her?"

Riley didn't know what to say. "I'm going to find her."

"You looked online. What else is there?"

She pressed her sweaty palms against her jeans. "There was a missing poster on my computer last night."

Shelby's mouth dropped open, but she didn't say anything.

"I have to find out about Jane, Shelby. I have to know—if she's me."

"So go home and ask your parents. Ask to see your birth certificate—*after* we get home. What can you do about it now anyway? It's not like you're going to find Jane O'Leary in the university library or something."

Riley felt butterflies flapping in her stomach. "We're going to be near the train station. I can take the train to Oregon. To Granite Cay."

Shelby's eyes narrowed. "That's the stupidest thing I've ever heard."

Riley felt suddenly deflated. Then baby Jane, smiling, slapping the water in her dream, flashed in her mind. "Will you at least cover for me?"

Shelby blew out a long sigh. "Do you even have a plan?"

Riley held up the folded birth certificate and even without opening it, she knew that Shelby knew exactly what it was.

"And if it's true? If you're really Jane and your parents stole you, what then?"

Riley's stomach turned over, the bile itching the back of her throat. She didn't want to consider what happened after; she just wanted to find Jane Elizabeth.

• • •

Riley clutched her backpack on her lap, waiting for the bus to lurch to a stop. Mrs. Carter clutched the bus seats as she walked, silently counting. Riley got up the second the teacher turned and started talking to someone.

"Where are you going?" Shelby hissed, one hand on the hem of Riley's sweatshirt.

Riley shook her off. "So Carter doesn't count me. Tell her my mom drove me in, but I'll be riding the bus back."

Generally, the security at Hawthorne High—and for all school events—was top notch. But Mrs. Carter had recently been divorced, lost seventy pounds, and dyed her hair an awful shade of burnt sienna that completely clashed with her too-small eyes. Everyone knew she had her sights set on blowing off Hawthorne and would have, had a teacher not been killed last year. Things were shuffled, teachers were moved, and Mrs. Carter stayed on, greeting her students every morning with unmasked disdain. On Mondays, she made an effort, and Riley and her class were weighed down with SAT vocab lists and reading assignments. By Friday, she was racking up points on her Words with Friends game, and as long as her students shuffled their papers to the front of the room and kept decently quiet, they were pretty much on their own.

If Mrs. Carter didn't want us in her classroom, Riley reasoned, *she sure as hell didn't want us on this bus trip.*

"Let me guess," Shelby whispered before letting Riley go. "Wise words from JD?"

Riley didn't answer—she was trying to remember the exact strategy JD had whispered in her ear twenty minutes ago—and Shelby groaned. "Just don't come to me for bail money."

Riley shouldered her backpack and shimmied to the back of the bus, grabbing for the restroom door.

OCCUPIED.

Damn it.

She slammed her fist against the door and eyed Mrs. Carter as she continued her walk-and-count, stopping every few seats to look up from her iPhone. Riley considered just going back to her seat. Shelby was right—Riley wasn't a sleuth, and her last stab at reckless adventure had been learning to skateboard without wearing a helmet. She bit her lip, looking at the back of her vacated seat then eyeing the closed bathroom door. Maybe fate was telling her to forget about it…

Defeated, Riley dropped her hands to her sides and spun to return to her seat, her boring adventureless life, but the bus lurched, slamming her backward. She tried to regain her footing but was instantly flung forward. Riley saw the red OCCUPIED sign coming directly at her and tried to throw up her hands, to do something to block the thing from being permanently stamped onto her forehead, but her hands were twisted on the straps of her backpack.

She was going down face-first directly in front of a rental bus's bathroom. If skipping out with JD didn't get her killed, flopping down there would.

"Ge—" Riley didn't get to finish her howl—or taste bus bathroom linoleum—because the door swung open and she fell right inside, right up against—

"JD!"

They were chest-to-chest, one of his arms wrapped around Riley, his palm at her lower back. His other hand was at his chin, index finger pressed against his upturned lips. "Shhh," he coaxed, as he pulled the bathroom door shut.

Riley straightened quickly, heat going from the soles of her feet to the top of her head.

JD was grinning a wicked, cocky grin, and Riley pressed her back up against the door, doing her best to put as much space between them as possible.

"I have to say I'm a little bit surprised to see you. But a little part of me"—he held his thumb and forefinger a quarter-inch apart—"knew you'd come."

Riley scrunched up her forehead in her best *as if* expression and crossed her arms in front of her chest. She planted her feet to avoid another crash into JD's surprisingly solid chest. "Maybe I just had to go to the bathroom, you pervert."

JD jutted his chin toward Riley's backpack. "With all that?"

Anger snaked up her spine. "It's none of your—"

"Shut up," JD whispered, head cocked.

"How dare–"

JD's eyes flashed, and Riley snapped her mouth shut, hearing Mrs. Carter's shuffling feet right outside the door. "Now remember our meet-up spots, everyone," she was saying in her already-exhausted voice. "Go directly to the lettered tables to pick up your group."

JD paused for a beat then grinned. Riley remembered that grin from detention. Even as they sat in the classroom in dead silence, JD was always snaking things from the teacher's desk when her back was turned or hacking into some computer system under the guise of homework. His eyes would go innocent and wide when he was suspected—then he would flash that smirk at Riley when he was cleared. It was warm and familiar…and she kind of liked it.

"So am I really to believe that the goody-goody Riley Spencer is skipping out on the college tour?" He went palms up. "Oh, wait. I meant the goody-goody Riley Spencer was bringing her luggage to take a pee. That makes more sense"

A little ripple of annoyance roiled through her. Riley straightened her shirt and put a hand on her hip. "I'm not that goody-goody. I was in detention too, you know."

"I know, Sleeping Beauty. So." JD raised his eyebrows and jutted his chin toward the outside. "Riding the rails, Riley Spencer?"

Riley's mind ticked. She thought about the birth certificate, about the fact that she had no plan whatsoever. She thought about Shelby and her "this isn't who you are" speech. She shrugged nonchalantly. "It's no big deal. I do it all the time."

JD seemed vaguely interested. "Oh yeah? So who you going to go see? Got some boyfriend out here?"

"If you must know, I'm going to see my friend."

"Your friend—?"

"Jane." Riley just spit it out, surprising even herself.

JD nodded, impressed. "Be sure to tell your friend Jane that I said hi."

"I will." Riley turned and went for the door.

"Not yet," JD said, looking far too comfortable sitting on the tiny sink. "Wait for the bus to clear. The driver will be last."

They dropped into silence, JD pulling a curl-edged book from the inside of his jacket. He began reading.

Riley glanced at the fake wood paneling up the walls of the restroom. It was everywhere, from ceiling to floor. It made the space look small. Too small.

Her chest was tightening, her breath becoming strained. Her eyes shot from corner to corner, desperate for a way out.

Not now, not now, not now, she commanded herself.

But the walls weren't listening. Panic started to rise in her chest, began to blot out the little bit of breath she was getting.

"What's wrong?" JD whispered, actual concern in his gold-flecked eyes.

Riley shook her head, unable to answer, unable to get enough air into her lungs to make a sound. Her fingers and toes started to tingle; her eyes started to water. Every one of her joints felt weighted down. She couldn't move. She was in a coffin, weighted air pinning her arms to her sides. She felt a tear roll over her cheek.

"No, no," JD said, closing the distance between them. "Don't do that. Don't panic."

But the walls were closing in. Everything was getting darker, pushing against her. She clawed at her chest, at her neck. Oh God, she couldn't breathe. She opened her mouth but nothing came out. *I should run,* she thought. *I can turn around and open the door and run.*

Riley did her best to turn around. She knew the door was there—*it had to be there.*

Tighter. The walls. Her breath.

Suddenly, there were arms around her. JD crushed her to his chest, pressing her head into his neck. She felt his lips at the part of her hair. She felt his feet pushing hers as he spun her around, yanking the tiny rectangle window open.

Riley tried to push back. The window made it worse. The screen was a tight metallic mesh that mocked her, assured her that she'd never get out. When she saw the blade, her panic had consumed her, was paralyzing every brain cell and synapse.

She was sure she was moving her lips, sure she was asking questions, but the blood thundered through her ears, blocking everything out. JD's arm went over her shoulder, the blade tight in his fist.

Her heart slammed against her ribcage. Her lungs burned, desperate for her to breathe. She watched the glistening steel blade slice through the window screen, making an X through it. Somewhere, the knife clattered into the sink, the screen was torn away, and Riley was pushed toward the now open window.

"Breathe, Riley," JD commanded.

She did as she was told, sucking in a huge gulp of outside air that inflated her lungs but still made them burn. It wasn't enough.

"It's OK, Riley. You're OK. You're OK. Keep breathing."

Another tortured breath. A slow burn.

She turned to JD, her eyes huge and glassy. He immediately pulled her into him, his lips against her ear.

"It's OK. Listen to my heartbeat. Do you hear it?"

She nodded dumbly, unable to do anything else.

"OK," JD whispered. "Think about that. My heart. Your heart. Now take a breath."

Riley did as she was told, the action becoming rote.

"That's right. In, out."

It was becoming easier to breathe. Riley's lungs opened up and the weight on her chest lessened. Pins and needles shot through her extremities, and she slowly unclenched fists that she didn't remember making. The walls stopped their slow drift inward. She sprang back from JD, embarrassed.

"I'm sorry," she muttered, dragging the back of her hand against her cheeks.

"Don't be. Panic attack, nothing to be ashamed of."

Claustrophobia, Riley thought, unwilling to correct him. She cleared her throat.

"Didn't you get the memo? This is high school. We're supposed to be ashamed of everything."

JD grinned. "I forgot you were kind of funny, Spence."

Riley shoved JD aside and squinted out the paperback-sized window, now void of a screen. "We're at the university." She spun toward the door. "We should go before—"

JD shrugged. "You can go whenever you want." He pulled a black backpack out from somewhere and grinned that stupid smile of his, that smile that was somehow familiar and calming, then shimmied around her. "Bus is empty."

Riley grabbed her bag and hurried behind him, still whispering. "How do you know it's clear?"

He looked over his shoulder. "Six-hour ride and the Marlboro man without a smoke? It's as clear as it's going to get."

A wisp of smoky air curled in through one of the open bus windows, and Riley felt her eyebrows go up. JD knew his stuff.

The train station was directly across from the university, and Riley tried to mimic JD's nonchalant gait, even as her blood pulsed through her body and her heart thudded in her throat.

She glanced over her shoulder just before she and JD reached the station, just before she pulled open the door. Behind her, the university greens lolled and college students hung out with books and friends, looking Norman Rockwell–wholesome. Riley gulped heavily and felt her skin tighten when a black-and-white police car pulled in front of the stopped bus, doing a slow crawl around the U-shaped drive.

She wondered if her mother called them.

She wondered if they were looking for her.

Then Riley wondered absently *which* mother was looking. The thought was errant, out of nowhere, but stabbed Riley in the gut.

I'm Riley Allen Spencer, she reminded herself, *and I'm being a total drama queen.*

Her own inner voice sounded off. Riley Allen Spencer sounded like a stranger. The realization hit like a fist in Riley's gut, and JD eyed her. "You OK?"

She cut her eyes to the train station in front of her then back to the university behind. "Let's just go in."

The inside of the station looked like it hadn't been touched in fifty years—but in a good way. The walls were covered with ornate woodwork, the floors some sort of granite or marble, buffed to a shine. She heard the click-clack of every footfall as people pushed past her, walking with purpose, knowing exactly where they needed to go. Riley stumbled backward, feeling even more like a child than she usually did.

Riley watched as JD strode right up to the lady in the booth. Within twenty seconds, the lady was laughing in a sweet, flirty way and pressing a ticket through the window toward him. Riley didn't see him go to his wallet.

Riley turned and studied the train map so JD wouldn't see her staring.

"You're up, cupcake."

Riley felt her eyes narrow. "I'm not your cupcake. And this is where our fun ends."

An easy smile slid across his lips. "So you admit we're having fun."

"Miss? Do you need a ticket? You've only got seven minutes before the next train."

"Oh, right. Sorry."

Riley sucked in a breath and felt her heart pound in her chest. *Why was I so nervous to buy a stupid train ticket?* "One ticket to Granite Cay, please," she said in her best fake-confidence voice.

"Round trip?" the woman asked.

Riley flushed. "Um, yeah. Do you know when the train comes back here?"

The woman smiled and pressed a train schedule and Riley's ticket through the slot in the window. Riley's hands shook as she grabbed it. *Get a grip! It's just a stupid train ticket! That will lead me to baby Jane Elizabeth—and my parents?*

That. Is. Not. My. Birth Certificate. I am Riley Spencer. I'm not some stolen, milk carton kid.

But maybe Jane Elizabeth was. She didn't know why she felt such a pull toward this baby, toward this mystery, but she couldn't dismiss it. Even when she slept, the baby and the birth certificate hung on the edge of her dreams.

And this was an adventure—something she would normally never do.

Electricity spiked through Riley, and that was probably why she didn't notice the guy behind her. She turned, ticket tucked safely in her coat pocket, and smacked into him. "Oh," she said, feeling her cheeks go hot and red. "Sorry."

The man smiled kindly, his eyes taking Riley in from head to toe. He had a fatherly air about him, and she felt that little niggling of guilt. "Going to see my parents," she sputtered to this perfect stranger.

He nodded, slight surprise in his eyes, and stepped around her.

Riley pushed away, still feeling the heat on her neck. When her cell phone blared out, she thought she would jump out of her skin.

"Oh, hi, hey, Mom."

"Ry, you were supposed to call me the minute you got off the bus." Her mother's voice was slow and stern, and dread dropped low in Riley's gut.

Just go back...

"And then I reminded your mother that this was your first trip with all your friends, and you were probably just getting shoveled off the bus and picking up your luggage. Right, turnip?" It was her father and his voice was cheery and friendly—and it sent guilt pinballing throughout Riley's brain.

She cleared her throat and edged herself into a quieter nook. "Yeah, that's right. I'm sorry, guys, I screwed up. I was a little crazy because we just got off the bus."

"So, you're at the university now? Have you gone in yet?"

Riley turned and faced the university stretching through every window in the train station vestibule. "Here. Haven't gone in yet," she repeated.

"Well, have a great time," her father said, getting back on the line.

"And be safe!" she heard her mother call from the background. "Don't talk to strangers or wander away from the group or—"

"Your mother says to have a wonderful time and don't run off with any boys or get any piercings or tattoos. At least no new ones."

Riley looked at her shoes, wishing she could laugh with her dad, but the angst—and the guilt—was too tight. "Thanks, Dad," she mumbled.

"Say hello to the ole alma mater. Love you, turnip."

Riley's breath hitched as her father mentioned the "alma mater" that he never attended.

"Love you too, Dad."

Riley held the phone to her ear even as the line went dead. She was lying to her parents. She slid her phone off and jammed it in her pocket, feeling the edge of the birth certificate jabbing into her palm.

My parents are lying to me.

FOUR

Riley took a deep, steadying breath and turned her back on the university. "Sorry, that was just—" Riley paused then spun around again, blinking, confused. "JD?" She took a few steps, her feet echoing loudly on the tiled floors, reverberating through the high ceilings. "JD?"

"Hey." He appeared behind Riley, and she clutched her chest, startled.

"I thought I lost you."

JD quirked an eyebrow, cocking his head. "I was headed for my train."

Riley nodded dumbly then JD pointed over her shoulder. "Your train is that way."

"We're on different trains?"

"Of course. We're going different places. And this is my train here. Have a nice trip—"

"Don't call me cupcake," Riley barked, holding up a hand.

JD turned, his hands on the straps of his backpack. Riley thought she heard him say "feisty" under his breath.

"OK." Riley turned and scanned the arches that led to the train platforms. Annoying as he was, she kind of wished she and JD were taking the same train. "See ya." She glanced down at her ticket again then up at the platforms. Not a single number on the platforms matched a single number on her ticket. She bit her lip, her nerves starting to thrum just under her skin.

"Granite Cay. Now boarding for Granite Cay. Train number 63 on platform 6. Now boarding…" The polite overhead voice faded off as Riley rushed to the platform, disappearing into the throng of people crowding onto the car.

Once she was seated, Riley pulled out her Kindle in a feeble attempt to quiet her mind. She felt like a rebel, a spy. She felt like she was doing something naughty and dangerous, and the thunk of her heart felt *good*.

Riley Spencer: bad girl. Free.

She smiled to herself and halfheartedly watched the rest of the people file onto the train—a mother yanking her school-aged daughter by the arm, a slew of businessmen each more gray tweed than the next, and the man Riley had run into in the vestibule. He walked past her, offering not a smile but a pleasant enough expression, and Riley felt heat bloom in her cheeks. She hoped he'd move on to the next train car but she didn't dare crane her head to look.

When the train lurched to a slow start, there were still people clogging the aisle ways, and Riley hugged her backpack to her chest while people plopped into every vacant seat. The man from the vestibule wandered back and sat in the seat across the aisle from her, looking straight ahead.

A tight fist of panic squeezed her heart.

Is he keeping tabs on me? Following me? Does he know my parents? Do my parents know I'm sneaking around?

The man pulled out a newspaper and unfolded it dramatically then buried his head and read.

You're an idiot, Riley. Lots of people bought tickets in Boone and then got on this train. Get. A. Grip.

She plugged her earphones into her tablet and pulled up a playlist, turning the music up loud. She flopped her head back and tried to close her eyes, but her body was still humming with excitement—and anxiety.

What if her parents knew someone on this train?

Riley glanced around as carefully as she could, doing her best to scrutinize every face, trying to catalogue them: were they looking at her? Had they ever shopped at her father's store? She was gripping the armrests, static whirring in her ears. She couldn't remember when her playlist ended.

"Hey. Hey!"

Riley blinked and straightened up, immediately wincing at the crick in her neck.

"JD?"

She sat up, panicked, and slapped her palm to her forehead. "Did I get on the wrong train? Oh my—"

JD shot her a nonchalant half smile. "No, you're fine. Doing what you do best."

She scrunched up her face, not understanding. "Riding the train?"

"No. Sleeping." He smiled and Riley rolled her eyes.

I wasn't sleeping, Riley wanted to say—but she caught herself before "I was studying everyone on the train" rolled out.

"What are you doing here?" Riley gripped the armrests and peeked out the windows. "And why are we stopped?"

"Well, we're stopped because we're here, and I'm here because"—he looked down quickly, his eyes avoiding hers—"I'm pretty sure you don't ride the train all the time."

Riley felt her stomach flop. "That obvious, huh?"

JD held his thumb and forefinger a millimeter apart. "Little bit. Especially since I've never seen you at the train station back home."

"We have a train station back home?"

"Across the street from the mall. Nice place; only smells like pee on two platforms. Remind me to take you on a tour someday. You ready?"

She followed him off the train and squinted in the bright sun. "How long did the ride take? Did I sleep the whole way? And hey, if you got on the train, where were you the whole time?"

"Ry, the way you sleep, I could have crawled into your lap and taken a nap right there and you would never have noticed."

"How do you know how I sleep?"

He yanked a Blow Pop from his jeans pocket, unwrapped it slowly, and popped it in his mouth. "You fell asleep in detention more than once or twice."

A little flutter went through Riley like an electric shock that tickled her palms and the soles of her feet. She told herself it was her shame at nodding off in the middle of school, but when she glanced at JD's sure smile out of the corner of her eye, she worried it was more.

"I have a boyfriend, you know." She blurted it out then immediately regretted it. She had no reason to lie to JD—especially not such a stupid lie about an imaginary boyfriend.

JD looked slightly confused. "OK. Then I won't ask you to suck my Blow Pop." He grinned, showing off perfect teeth tinged slightly blue by the pop.

"I was just saying…"

"All right, cupcake, where we headed?"

"What about your concert?"

JD waved at the air. "No big. I've seen 'em a hundred times. A girl lost in the big city? Never seen that before."

Riley crossed her arms in front of her chest. "You're an ass, you know." But even as the words escaped her lips, Riley knew she was lying. Every inch of her was glad that JD was there.

"OK, so which way to Jane's house?"

"What?"

"Your friend, Jane." JD paused, his eyebrows going up. "Wait, there is no Jane, is there?"

Riley felt the butterflies in her stomach again. She was in Granite Cay. She was close to Jane Elizabeth O'Leary—whoever she was.

JD was staring her down with his no-nonsense eyes. "Out with it."

Riley swallowed.

"Hey, if I'm skipping a Death to Sea Monkeys concert for this…"

They were still standing on the train platform, and the Granite Cay Hospital was directly across the road from them.

"Let me guess: we're here to visit your crazy mother in the psych ward?"

Riley smiled despite herself. "I really can't believe that you and Shelby Webber don't get along better." She paused when his expression didn't change. "OK. No psycho mother, but I do have to go into the hospital to look up some records. Totally boring stuff. You want to grab a coffee or something and meet up later?"

JD shifted his weight. Something flitted across his face—hurt?—but was gone just as quickly. "Do you not want me to go with you?"

"No, it's not that," she lied, hiking up her already hiked-up backpack. "It's just that, you know, hospitals. Gross. People die there."

"What do you need from the records room?"

Riley had her hands in the pocket of her hoodie, her left hand repeatedly touching the birth certificate as if to assure herself it was still there—that this was all real. The paper was so soft it was almost clothlike, and when Riley looked into JD's clear, earnest eyes, she almost wanted to spit out the whole thing. But she held back. Riley wasn't sure what she'd find in the hospital records, and she wasn't sure what it would mean for her or for Jane.

I can't betray her for a hot guy with nice eyes and a rap sheet, she thought.

She shrugged. "Just some family stuff. You know, medical histories and all."

"Can't your doctor just have them email it?"

Riley opened her mouth, stumped. "Uh, no." She rushed on. "The files are really old and they're not digitized yet. So…I said I'd go in. So, I'll meet you when I'm done?"

JD pursed his lips. "One sec. I just want to get this straight.

68

You tell your parents you're going on a college tour and they, what? Said, 'hey, just in case you happen to ditch the university thing and catch a train four hours away to Granite Cay, could you pick up some medical records for us?' Something like that?"

"Um, yes?"

He swung his head. "Not buying it."

"Look, I'm just looking up some stuff for a friend." Riley's mind raced, images of the birth certificate, her web search, the black-and-white photo of the chubby baby from the HAVE YOU SEEN ME? picture bombarding her. "She was adopted."

"Jane?"

"Yeah, Jane. She was adopted and she's looking for her birth parents. I said I'd help her out." She looked over her shoulder, trying to seem nonchalant, but certain the jerky action just solidified the fact that she was lying through her teeth. "Jane was born in Granite Cay, so this was all a—a happy accident." She forced a placating smile.

"Yeah, sure. Whatever." JD jerked his head toward a tiny coffee house on their side of the street. "Do you want me to grab you something? Something nonfat and girlie?"

Riley put her hands on her hips. "Nonfat?"

JD took a step back and blew out an exasperation-tinged sigh. "I didn't mean anything by it, I swear. Just come get me when you're done."

• • •

The hospital lobby was freezing, and Riley zipped up her hoodie and shuddered.

"I know," said the lady at the front desk, meeting Riley's eyes. She was wearing scrubs with cartoon kitties all over them and a nametag that said Carla. "The air conditioner is stuck. Perfectly healthy people are walking in off the street and getting a bed!" She laughed at her own joke, her boobs, which were the size of Riley's head, jiggling with the effort. "Can I help you with something, missy?"

"Um." It came out a pitiful squeak and Riley cleared her throat. "There was a baby born here."

"Well, honey, maternity is on the third floor."

"No, not a—I need to find a record on a baby that was born here."

Carla's penciled-in eyebrows rose into her tight black curls. "A baby?"

Riley pulled the birth certificate from her pocket. "She may have been adopted."

Carla sighed and leaned closer to Riley, pushing her elbows onto the desk. "Look, honey, I understand what you're going through, but I can't just go handing over those records. There must have been a reason why the adoptive parents asked for a closed adoption. I know it's hard, honey." Carla reached out and patted Riley's hand; Riley stared down at the intricate pattern on Carla's incredibly long fingernails and absently wondered how she typed. "But it was probably the best thing all around."

Riley's expression sunk, and Carla pursed her lips into a tight pucker. "Did you want to do it? Did your parents make you do it? Make you give up your baby? Lord, you wouldn't be the first who came back looking for their child. You're awfully young though, aren't ya?"

Riley stepped back, shaking her head. "No. Oh, no." She pushed the birth certificate toward Carla. "It wasn't my baby. I didn't have it. It—she—" Riley pointed to the page as if the complete explanation was written there.

Carla smoothed the paper, her pursed pucker breaking into a soft smile. "Is this you, honey? Were you the one who was adopted?"

Riley's mouth went dry.

"*Your parents probably stole you…*" Shelby's words echoed in her head—but this time, the lightness in them was gone. *Could I be baby Jane? Could I have been adopted?* Riley tried to swallow. *Or stolen?* Again, her mind raced. She didn't have asthma; her father did. Her mother burned if she so much as stepped into direct sunlight—Riley never burned. They were fiercely overprotective. They never let her go out alone. And the one thought that hit Riley like a punch to the gut: there were no pictures of her before the age of three.

Because she hadn't been there.

"Hon?"

Riley cleared her throat. "Yeah…I guess."

Carla tilted her head and her eyebrows rose into sympathetic slits. "Oh, honey. It goes both ways. I can't give you any information unless you have ID. Does your ID have"—she took the page between her enormous fingernails—"Jane Elizabeth O'Leary on it?"

Riley shook her head. "Can you at least—can you at least tell me if you have any records on any of these people? Like, did they come in later for a broken bone or chicken pox or something? Did they have any big illnesses?"

Carla looked at Riley, head still cocked, ruby red lips pressed in a contemplative pucker. She looked all around her then leaned in close again. "I shouldn't be doing this, but since I've been telling them to fix the dag-on air conditioning for two months now and they ain't done nothing about it, I can take a small liberty."

Riley sucked in a breath, sure that an enormous, stupid grin was cutting across her whole face. Carla paused then and eyed her. "Just a small one. I can tell you if the family has been through here."

Riley's heart pattered nervously as Carla heaved herself back into her chair and focused hard on the computer monitor in front of her. "Lemme see that paper again, honey."

Riley slipped the birth certificate over the counter and clasped her hands behind her back so Carla wouldn't see them trembling. She looked over Carla's head, studying everything on every wall while Carla typed and Riley's heart leapt into her throat. She was about to start pacing when Carla said, "Hmm. Now that's odd." She picked up the paper and squinted at it, pulled a pair of cheater eyeglasses up her nose, and typed again. She threw herself back in her chair and it squeaked a few inches backward. "Hmm."

"Is everything OK?"

Carla folded up the birth certificate and handed it back to Riley. "I'm sorry, honey, but there is no record of this birth in our system."

There was a tightness in Riley's chest that spread slowly, heavily, through her whole body. "What?"

Carla shook her head. "Birth certificate says the baby was born here, but no, I don't have any record of it at all. Kind of like a phantom."

Riley leaned forward, rolling up on her tiptoes, her fingers gripping Carla's counter so hard they were white. "But what about the parents? Did you look them up?"

Carla clucked and shook her head some more. "Tried 'em all. Even different spellings, you know, 'cuz a lot of times people get nervous just after they get their babies. But nothing." She shrugged, her big shoulders hugging her ears. "Nada."

"Well, maybe your records just don't go back far enough."

"Nope. I've got records of births seven years before this one. I'm sorry, honey, but maybe you weren't born here after all."

"Well, is there another Granite Cay Hospital? Maybe it happened there and they got the—the addresses mixed up." Even as Riley said it, she knew how thin and desperate her explanation was. Carla knew too, and she patted Riley's hand again gently.

"I wish I could help you, honey, I really do, but there's nothing here."

Riley nodded slowly, her whole body feeling numb. The room was enormous but the walls started to creep toward her. She stepped away from Carla's counter and sat down hard on the closest chair she could find. It was grossly stained but she didn't care.

The baby wasn't born here. The parents didn't exist.

If it was a regular adoption, Riley reasoned, *there would be a paper trail. Unless her parents didn't want anyone to know…*

Her throat constricted. Her parents wouldn't do that. They wouldn't just steal a baby—or adopt one and hide the records. They were rule followers, a by-the-book family. They would have told her if she were adopted.

Riley unfolded the birth certificate again, scrutinizing it, just as she had nearly every hour since she'd found it. If it were true—if her parents *stole* her—would the hospital have no record? Did the hospital destroy her record in an effort to protect itself? Riley felt sick and sweaty, but she didn't want to be in that hospital for one minute longer.

She made a beeline for the automated glass doors and gulped greedily at the lukewarm, non-germ-infested air outside. She edged away from some smokers, and her heart seized when she saw a man peering at her. *I know him—I know him—I know him,* Riley thought, trying to shake her brain from its fog.

The train!

The second she remembered where she knew him from, he was gone, zigzagging across the hospital's well-manicured lawn and into the parking lot. He threw a glance over her shoulder and caught Riley's eye, his gaze so icy that she felt it zing through her.

Why was he here?

Riley considered flipping on her heel and asking Carla for a bed in the psych ward when her cell phone rang and nearly gave her a heart attack.

"Are you going to stand there all day or are you coming into the coffee place?"

Riley licked her lips, trying to pull her scattered thoughts back together. "Um, yeah. I mean, no. I'll be right over."

She crossed the street without looking and thanked God that her stupidity didn't turn her into a hood ornament. She took several deep breaths before yanking open the coffeehouse door. She chanced a glance over her shoulder, expecting the train man to be right behind her, his nose pushed up against the window, but the sidewalk was empty. She turned, scanning the place for JD.

"Hey."

He was sitting at a corner table, a spiral notebook open in front of him, its pages littered with his precise black scrawl. He pressed a coffee toward Riley and smiled. "It's full fat. Extra whipped cream."

She took the coffee and tried to mirror JD's smile. By the odd way he looked at her, Riley was pretty certain that her mirrored expression was a fun house one. She leaned over and sipped her coffee.

"Almond Roca?" Riley asked, letting the sweet warmth of the coffee slip through her.

"Shot in the dark," JD said with a shrug. "So, did you get what you needed at the hospital?"

Riley bit her bottom lip then frowned. "Actually, no."

"No? They didn't have Jane's medical records? How is that possible?"

Riley took a big swig of coffee, letting it burn her throat and buy her some time. "They had the records but they—they're not at the hospital anymore."

JD dropped his pen and leaned back in his chair, flexing his arms over his head. Riley looked away as his biceps stretched out the arms of his T-shirt. "You mean they're at the hall of records or something now?"

Hope bloomed in her gut. "Yes, hall of records. Carla—from the front desk—said I should go there now." Riley looked at JD's open notebook, at his still steaming coffee mug. "Or in a little bit."

He flipped his book closed. "Why wait?"

"Because I have no idea where to go, for starters."

JD sauntered over to the front counter and leaned in toward the barista. He gestured Riley over.

The barista drew a crude map on a paper napkin, explaining the busses they should take to get to the hall of records. Once they confirmed that they had it, the barista looked up at JD and then at Riley. "Whaddya'll want at the hall of records? They don't have anything there but ancient stuff."

"Actually, my friend is looking for fam—"

"Farming records," Riley interjected. "For a school project."

JD shot her a strange look but the barista didn't seem to notice. He just shrugged and pushed the napkin into Riley's hand. "Well, good luck."

"Farming records?" JD asked, his brow creased.

"I have my reasons. Look! That's the number 27 bus."

It took nearly twenty minutes of lurching stops and nondescript townscape before they reached the hall of records, which was also, ominously, the end of the line.

"Everyone off," the bus driver said.

"Everyone" was Riley and JD, and they did as they were told, blinking into the heavy sunshine as it glared off the enormous white-washed walls of the Granite Cay Hall of Records.

JD grabbed the door and swung it open for Riley. "Farming records await," he said, ushering her inside.

The nervous flutter was back, shooting through Riley's belly. She felt the coffee churn and prayed she wouldn't throw up. The hospital was a dead end. *But this will be it,* she told herself. *This is where all the records are.*

Riley stepped in and waited for JD, who let the door go behind her. "Hey." She caught the door before it closed and poked her head out. "Aren't you coming in?"

"I thought it was boring family stuff for Jane. You know, like at the hospital."

"Oh, yeah. Right."

Riley's heart thundered in time with the butterfly wings batting in her gut.

I'm not into JD—not at all, she told herself. *It was nice to have him on the train and nicer still that he came out to make sure I didn't end up taking a train to hell or the end of the world,* but suddenly she felt a little naked, a little alone—and a little uncomfortable.

"I was just asking."

JD held her eye for a beat then flipped open his notebook and sat on the heavy cement wall outside. "I'll be here when you're done."

Riley stepped into the hall of records, and the glass door snapped shut behind her. *Like a mausoleum door.* The thought was fleeting, and she convinced herself it was due to the white marble floors in front of her and the ornate stucco décor on the walls rather than the sudden feeling of breathlessness. Her chest was tight and her blood ran hot and heavy through her limbs.

Riley followed the signs to the help desk, her heels clacking on the marble, the sound reverberating through the halls in vague echoes. Her lips were pressed together, and she realized she was holding her breath. She shook herself and put on her warmest smile.

"Hello," Riley said to the woman behind the help desk. "I'm looking for some records regarding a baby that was born in this town? It was eighteen years ago and—"

The woman didn't look up from her magazine. "Mmm hmmm."

"I checked Granite Cay Hospital—where the girl was born—and they said to come here. This is her birth certificate." Riley unfolded the paper, smoothing it against the desk, and pushed it to the woman. The woman looked up, her dark eyes scanning Riley, then the page.

"Is this you?"

"No, but—"

"She family?"

Riley had seen enough television to know that family were generally the only people privy to this kind of information so she nodded, trying her best to look totally nonchalant. "Yep. Jane is my sister."

The woman scanned the birth certificate one more time, and then scanned Riley as if there was any connection to be made between the two. "What exactly are you looking for?"

"Just some record—where she lived, where she moved. That kind of thing."

The woman arched an eyebrow and Riley rushed on. "We—um—were adopted. Split up. My mother did drugs and we have different fathers and hers wasn't around so…" She forced a quaver in her voice and tried to remember the speech she had heard on some Lifetime movie about boxcar children or orphans or something. "I just want to find her so we can put our family back together."

Riley blinked back tears and saw the desk woman soften. "Oh, that's so sad. Well, where she lived could be public record in the census. You don't know who adopted her?"

"Well, no, not exactly. But I figured since I had her birth certificate, maybe there would be another copy here and that would tell me more."

Desk woman nodded. "It could." She pointed. "Go right back there. If it's only—what, eighteen years ago—it should be on the computers. If not, you can try the stacks. Otherwise, there's the microfiche, but she seems much too young to be there."

Riley licked her lips. "What about newspaper articles? I—I, uh, think I remember someone saying something about a big crime spree about the time she was born. Bank robbery or something." Riley was almost nervous about how easy it was becoming to fabricate a backstory for Jane.

"The stacks. If you need to photocopy anything, it's twenty-five cents a page, or ten cents a page to print anything out. Good luck."

Riley refolded the birth certificate and held herself back from running toward the computers and stacks.

Twenty minutes later, she had located every other baby born at Granite Cay Memorial Hospital on June 14, 1995, but no Jane Elizabeth. She had never registered for school, and her parents never owned a home or signed up for the census. It was like Jane and her family never existed at all.

Riley's finger hovered over the *Granite Cay Gazette*. The idea of Jane—of Riley herself as Jane—was weighing heavily on her now. Jane and her family didn't exist. But the birth certificate proved she did once. And it was hidden—locked away in *Riley's* baby book. Her stomach soured and she chewed the inside of her cheek. Could her parents—? She looked back at the computer screen.

If Jane had been kidnapped, there would be an article about it. If something horrible had happened to the family—murdered, killed in a car crash—it would be in the *Gazette*.

She blew out a long sigh and typed in Granite Cay—Major Crime—1995–1998. Her stomach burned, and it seemed like the ancient hall of records computers were deliberately taking hours, ratcheting up her own tension. Finally a slew of articles populated the screen, each one stabbing at Riley.

If she was Jane—if her parents stole her—what did that mean for her? For them?

She clicked on the first article, the tightness in her heart becoming unbearable—until she read the headline: "Major Crimes Division Breaks Car Thief Ring." She clicked to the next: "Drugs Found in High School Student's Locker." She rested her chin in her hands, clicking article after article on small-time crimes that the city of Granite Cay considered major. There wasn't a single kidnapping mentioned, the only death an eighty-nine-year-old woman in a house fire. Somewhere, a band of graffitiing teenagers ran amok.

"Were you planning on leaving me there all day?"

Riley snapped up when she heard JD's voice then immediately regretted it when her neck started to spasm. She rubbed the aching spot just under her ear. "Oh, I'm sorry. I guess time got away from me."

"Well, that's understandable." JD squinted. "What with this

fascinating report of suspected score tampering at the Sixth Annual Dolphin Swim Tournament." He feigned terror. "Where the Granite Cay Water Bonnets took second place for the third year in a row. What the hell is a water bonnet? Are they seriously named after hats?"

Riley was too exhausted—and annoyed—to be amused. She thunked her forehead on the desk in front of her. "Ugh. I'm sorry. And this was a big waste of time too. I couldn't find a single thing I was looking for."

"Well, yeah, if you're looking for medical records in the *Gazette*."

"Do you have a better idea?"

"Yeah. Pizza."

"How is pizza going to help me find…medical records?"

"It's not, but it'll help me from dying of starvation." He grinned and she couldn't argue; her stomach growled at the thought of a big, greasy pie.

They found a diner a block away from the hall of records and slid into a booth. "If you're getting a roasted veggie with no cheese, I'm out," JD said, scanning the menu.

Riley wrinkled her nose. "What is a roasted veggie with no cheese?"

"It's a pizza."

"No, it's not. An all-meat supreme with extra cheese and double sauce is a pizza."

JD shut his menu and grinned. "My kind of woman."

After the waitress took their order, JD leaned back in his seat and eyed Riley. Riley immediately felt self-conscious. "What?"

"Are you ever going to tell me why we're really out here?"

Riley looked around the restaurant. "We're out here because you're starving."

"In Granite Cay, Ry. Who's Jane and what are you looking for?"

FIVE

Nerves like steel bands wound around Riley's heart. She tried to swallow but found her mouth was dry. She looked into JD's eyes and thought about their detention week. He was funny; he was nice—he was smart. She licked her lips.

"I really don't know who Jane is. I came here trying to find out."

To her surprise, JD didn't laugh. "OK. So if you don't know who she is, where did you get the name?"

The birth certificate was burning in Riley's pocket. She took a deep breath and slid the paper across the table. She scrutinized JD as he opened the folded paper, his hazel eyes scanning it, then meeting hers.

"This is a birth certificate."

Riley nodded. "I know."

"For Jane. But you don't know who she is."

"No."

"She must be someone pretty important if you're willing to hop a train and come all the way out here for her."

Riley swallowed. "You hopped a train and came all the way out here."

The waitress broke in, sliding an enormous pizza in between them. She turned away and JD already had a giant bite of pizza in his mouth. He swallowed. "So you have no idea who Jane Elizabeth O'Leary is?"

Riley pulled a slice of pizza onto her plate but couldn't bring herself to eat. "I've been trying to figure that out, but I keep coming up empty."

Recognition flashed across JD's face. "The hospital, the hall of records."

"I couldn't find anything." She picked at an ancient glob of cheese stuck to the Formica table. "So, I—I'm beginning to think that Jane Elizabeth O'Leary is me. I'm her."

She waited for JD to drop his pizza or reel in stunned silence. She waited for him to grab his phone and dial 9-1-1.

Instead, he took another huge bite and asked, "So you're adopted?"

Riley's mind was blazing. "No," she said quickly. "No, I wasn't adopted. That's not even my birth date."

"So then you're not Jane."

Riley was getting exasperated. "I think I *was* Jane."

"So your parents changed your name and your birth date? That's weird. Why would they do that?"

"Exactly. Why would they?" She looked around, suddenly feeling very exposed. She dropped her voice to a hoarse whisper. "I think I may have been kidnapped."

JD stopped chewing and put his slice on his plate. "Why do you think that?"

"I found this birth certificate hidden in a slit in my baby book. I'm almost positive it's me. I don't even look like my parents. They won't let me do anything. I had to beg for a month to get them to let me on the school trip to look at colleges."

JD looked around the pizza parlor. "Well, in hindsight…"

"You know what I mean!"

"So all that adds up to kidnapping but not to adoption."

Riley grabbed the slice from her plate and took a big bite. "My parents would have told me if I was adopted."

"Because the parents who you think are kidnappers, who changed your name and your birth date, wouldn't lie to you."

Riley chewed her pizza, considering. "I know it sounds weird, but I know them. I know I'm not adopted. We talked about adoption all the time. The family across the street from our old house adopted a kid from Vietnam. We were friends with them. I remember having a conversation with my dad, though, before Thuy came home. I asked him how I could make the little girl feel welcome and he didn't say, 'you can tell her you were adopted too.'"

JD picked up his slice again. "Well, that seals it. You, Riley Spencer slash Jane O'Leary, were kidnapped because your father *didn't* say you were adopted."

Riley threw down her pizza. "I knew I shouldn't have told you. You're a real ass, you know that?"

"OK, OK, I'm sorry, Ry. It's just kind of a big thing to wrap your head around, isn't it? There have to be a million other explanations for that birth certificate."

"The bigger thing is that nothing came up at the hospital or at the hall of records. Even if baby Jane isn't me, why did this family just disappear, and how would my parents be involved?"

JD straightened. "Involved? Like, you think your parents may have made Jane's parents disappear?"

Riley put her chin in her hands, frowning. "I don't know what I think anymore."

"Well, you said you found the birth certificate in your baby book. Don't you have pictures of yourself as a baby with your parents? My parents have them all over the house. It's ridiculously embarrassing."

Riley warmed, thinking of JD as a smiling, round baby in the arms of his doting parents. But the thought was immediately replaced by something cold and dark. "There aren't any pictures of me as a baby. Nothing until I was about three."

JD sipped his Coke. "Really?"

Riley started to feel clammy and panicky again. "Not a single one. My parents said that the house we used to live in flooded and we pretty much lost everything. That's why my mom started making the new baby book."

"Do you remember anything about the old house?"

Riley tried to remember. "No, I don't think so. I mean, I kind of remember the layout, but I'm not sure if it's because that's what they told me, you know? It was in Chicago, I remember that—I think."

The pizza sat in Riley's gut like a heavy black stone. Heat snaked up the back of her neck and suddenly everything—the pizza parlor, the booth, her clothes—felt wrong. *Who am I?* she thought, the panic pinballing through her.

"Do you remember anything about Chicago?" JD was asking.

Riley shook her head, everything going in super slow motion. "Only what they've told me."

JD blew out a sigh, and Riley held his eye, tears threatening to well in hers. She didn't know why it was so important that JD believe her. She didn't know why it seemed to ache that he looked at her with a slight, disbelieving grin on his face.

"You just don't understand. I used to know who I was. Now I have no idea. I don't know what's been a lie, what's real. I feel like I've been play-acting this whole time."

"Riley, there's nothing different about you. You're still the same person—you just found a birth certificate. And even if it is yours, it's not going to change who you are right now or any of your experiences in the past."

"But—"

JD reached out and put his hands on Riley's. "You are who you are, period. What you or other people expect you to be doesn't figure in to the equation. Jane or Riley—it doesn't matter. You're you."

Riley sat back, considering. She pasted on a contented smile for JD, all the while thinking, *But who am I?*

Riley dumped a few bills on the end of the table, wrestling her coat and backpack from the booth. "This was a mistake. I have to get back. This was so dumb."

"Ry! Ry!"

She heard JD's voice behind her, but it already sounded too far away.

I'm no one, Riley thought. *Maybe I don't exist at all.*

She slipped into a coffee shop and took a seat by the window, tucking herself against the wall while she pulled her laptop out of her backpack. She started it up, her hands flying over the keyboard.

RILEY ALLEN SPENCER.

The search immediately popped up a half-dozen other Riley Spencer's before she found a tiny mention of herself tucked between a professor and a mechanic.

Spencer, Riley. Sophomore.

It was a grainy school picture reprinted in the Hawthorne High *Hornet.* Riley was being quoted about a student and teacher who were murdered last year. It was a brainless, stock quote—"We're all a little more aware of each other"—that she couldn't remember saying. And her picture—she recognized herself but just barely. She looked like every other teenaged girl in a school photo in a school newspaper ever.

If she had been kidnapped, did her real family wonder what she looked like? Would they remember her? Would they recognize her? What was going on?

A sob choked in the back of her throat. She snapped her laptop shut and was startled to see JD sitting across from her, holding out her cell phone.

"You forgot this."

She reached for it, silently, but he didn't let it go. "You OK?"

Riley blew out a world-on-her-shoulders sigh. "Why would my parents be hiding a birth certificate in my baby book if it wasn't mine? And then, these people don't even exist?"

JD shook his head. "I have no idea, Ry. You should just ask

them." He reached over and brushed her cheek with his thumb. She didn't even know she was crying.

"Second time I had to do that today."

Riley sniffed and smiled. Something about JD—maybe it was the fact that he was a loner or that he didn't seem to care what anyone else thought—made her feel comfortable.

"You could just ask," he repeated.

"No. I wasn't supposed to be going through my mom's things when I found the baby book. And then I snooped through that. She'll be pissed at me."

JD sat back in his chair and kicked out his legs, crossing them at the ankles. "So just decide what's worse—your parents being pissed at you or you never knowing who Jane Elizabeth O'Leary is."

Riley chewed her bottom lip. Two days ago, finding Jane seemed like a fun adventure. Now it had turned into an obsession. She *had* to know.

"Here." JD pushed a white plate with an enormous chocolate chip cookie on it. "I find sugar is brain food."

Riley grinned, breaking off a piece. JD did the same and she knocked her cookie hunk against his. "Cheers."

"To solving mysteries?"

"Something like that." She popped the cookie piece in her mouth and chewed, very aware that JD's eyes were on her, studying her.

"What?" she asked, heat burning the tops of her earlobes.

JD looked at the table, but he was still smiling. "Nothing. I just never thought that I would have spent the afternoon skipping school with someone like you."

Riley's brows went up. "Someone like me?"

He broke off another bite of cookie. "A goody-goody."

She rolled her eyes. "And I never thought that I would be sitting in a café, sharing a giant cookie with a juvenile delinquent."

As soon as the words were out of Riley's mouth, she wanted to take them back. Something dark flashed in JD's eyes, but he tried to pass it off, digging into his wallet. All traces of his playful smile were gone as he dumped a few bills on the table.

"No—I didn't mean—"

JD stood. "What? It's nothing. I just feel like heading out now. I've got some things I want to do before I get back to Boone."

No more *we*, and Riley was stung.

"I didn't mean that I think you're a criminal or—"

But JD already had his back toward her, his backpack slung over one shoulder. "Later, Ry."

She watched, breathless, as he walked out the glass door, letting it slam shut behind him. She slapped her laptop shut and threw it into her backpack, trying her best to keep her eye on JD's retreating back as he beelined away from Riley.

"JD!" she called when she hit the sidewalk. "JD!"

He didn't turn and she was losing ground. She bolted into the street but didn't hear the screech until the grille of the car was just inches from her. Everything dropped into a paralyzing silence; everyone moved in slow motion.

She thought she heard someone say her name. She thought she felt hands on her shoulders, around her waist, people carrying her gingerly.

"Riley! Riley!" She blinked, and JD's face—eyes wide with concern—came into focus.

"I didn't hit her!" a woman was yelling, her voice high and hysterical. "She ran out into the street."

Riley was sitting in a metal chair though she had no idea how she got there. JD was crouched in front of her, holding both of her hands. She felt another hand tapping her shoulder gently.

"She wasn't hit, but she's rattled. Is there someone I can call for you? What's your name? I can call your parents for you."

Riley turned toward the man's voice. It was the guy from the train station, from the hospital—and now right here, on the street. He seemed to have a very faint accent, but Riley couldn't place it.

"Are you OK? I'm a doctor—"

She heard JD's voice. "She's fine, just a little stunned."

Riley hoped she was nodding her head, but everything felt totally disconnected—even her own limbs. Finally, she was able to force her lips to move. "I'm OK," she said, her voice small and breathy. "I'm sorry. It was my fault."

JD looked at her, his eyebrows pressed together. "Do you want me to call your parents?" he asked once the crowd had dispersed.

"That guy. The doctor. I saw him on the train and at the hospital."

JD nodded slowly, taking her hand and helping her up. Panic shot through the nothingness she felt a second ago. "I think he's following me."

"Riley, he's a doctor. He rides the train."

"But he was right here," Riley said, leaning in.

"This town is like four square miles. Of course you're going to run into him."

The sobs came out of nowhere.

"Ry—"

"I'm sorry. I don't know what's wrong with me."

"We'll just get you home and—"

The tears wracked her harder. "That's just it. What if I am Jane? What if—if my parents have been lying to me my whole life?" She shook her head, horrified at how ridiculous her fit was sounding. "Oh my God. This is so stupid. I'm just spazzing out. I should never have dragged you into this. Riley—Jane Elizabeth—both of us are unstable."

JD shook his head but smiled. "I'll be sure to mention both your personalities on the nuthouse intake form."

Riley rolled her eyes. "Then I'd start out being Jane Elizabeth." She sniffed. "The girl without a past."

He slung an arm across her shoulders. "And I'm the guy who can't escape his."

Heat flushed Riley's cheeks, but JD's smile was soft.

• • •

Everyone else on the bus was asleep except for Riley. JD was stretched across two seats, his heavy black boots sticking out into the aisle, his hands clasped behind his head. Shelby had a brand-new Hudson U sweatshirt balled up under her cheek and was quietly drooling onto the glossy satin D. Riley felt like she couldn't close her eyes even if she wanted to—like if she did, she might open them up again into a different life, a different person.

What if I am Jane?

The thought was heavy in her gut.

Do I have sisters and brothers? Would I have had a whole different life?

She thought about her parents—overprotective—but benign and sweet. Her father taught her to ride a bike. Her mother helped her paint her room.

But still the thought niggled at her.

This is crazy, Riley thought as the bus crossed the Welcome to Crescent City sign. She knew her parents. She trusted them. And she was a jerk for accusing them of being ruthless kidnappers.

But there are no pictures…

Her head lolled to the side, looking across the aisle where JD was lying, the faint light from outside casting spider-web shadows down his cheeks. He looked peaceful asleep. But suddenly, he blinked at her. Riley's heart did a little double thump and she saw his grin spread in the darkness.

"You OK?"

She shrugged. "Yeah, totally."

JD closed his eyes again but didn't stop smiling. "Lies. I can see it with my eyes closed."

Maybe it was the emotional exhaustion of the last two days, or that as of now, JD was just as close to Jane Elizabeth as Riley was, but she started talking. "I don't know. I just feel—"

"Silly? Crazy?" JD shrugged back at her. "Don't worry, it's no big deal. You have questions."

Riley worried her bottom lip and slipped her hands into her

sweatshirt sleeves. "Do you think they're out there looking for me? I mean, if it's true, you know?"

JD shifted in his seat so he was closer to her. "Ry, it's not that I don't believe you, but we looked. There were no missing kid reports that matched your description."

It was like a fist to her gut.

"That's right. If my parents snatched me, then no one was looking for me. No one cared that I was missing."

Before she knew it, Riley had slipped out of her seat and into JD's. His arm was around her and she was leaning into him, somehow comforted by the constant tick of his heart, the systematic rise and fall of his breath. She didn't consider what Shelby would say, what her parents would say—what every other person on the bus would say if they saw her curled into him, JD, the bad kid. It felt good to melt into his arms—into the arms of someone she could count on. She started. *Did I just say that I could count on JD?* She shook herself—or tried to. She was trembling, but she refused to cry.

He looked down at her, his eyes glittering in what remained of the light. "Maybe no one kidnapped you. Maybe there's another explanation."

"I don't want to think of my parents that way, but what other explanation is there? I have no baby pictures, no family, they keep me under lock and key. I'm willing to believe I was adopted—"

JD's eyebrows went up, slightly amused.

"—but there isn't even the slightest clue that I was adopted."

"Ry," JD whispered, "you don't have to figure everything out right now, OK? Give yourself another couple of hours to be Riley Spencer."

"Why should I do that?"

JD wouldn't look at her. "Because I was just beginning to really like her."

The bus lurched to a stop and the running lights went on. Everyone started to scramble, Riley included.

"Hey," Shelby said, her eyes clouded with sleep. "Did you sit somewhere else?"

Riley felt her cheeks flush red. She glanced over her shoulder at JD who was gathering up his backpack. "No," she said quickly. "I was here the whole time. You're just a heavy sleeper." She smiled thinly, the whole time her heart beating a steady rhythm: liar. Liar. Liar.

"Oh, I forgot to tell you. Cassia Lohmen went into labor tonight."

"Your neighbor?"

"Yeah. She asked me if I could come over and watch the girls overnight, so I won't be riding home with you. Her sister is going to come get me and drop me off on her way to the hospital. Do you think you could catch a ride home?"

Riley frowned. "Oh, yeah. OK." She thought of the long stretch of highway ahead of her—there was nothing for twenty miles between the high school and Riley's new housing development. It was desolate and blank. "I can just call my parents."

They shuffled off the bus.

"OK, I'm off to Cassia's." Shelby blew an air kiss. "And I still hate you for not telling me everything on the bus." She pulled

Riley close, her fingers wrapping around Riley's upper arm. "You're calling me first thing in the morning, right?"

Riley nodded, little pricks of heat going up her spine. She couldn't tell Shelby about JD—she kind of didn't want to. But she whispered, "Sure," anyway.

Shelby ran off and Riley fumbled in her purse, looking for her cell phone. She yanked out her makeup bag, her notebook, and was going for the phone when a folded piece of paper popped out of the depths of the bag and flopped onto the ground. She snatched it up and frowned. Another black-and-white postcard. This one was even more random—a little kid, maybe ten or so—blowing out birthday candles. There were other kids in the picture, most in profile, and a woman leaning toward the birthday boy. Her long hair shadowed most of her face. That was it.

Riley turned the card over, her breath hitching.

I KNOW WHO YOU ARE.

SIX

The words were carefully written in all capitals, same as the other postcard. Her fingers began to tremble.

She wanted to crumple the card. She wanted to tear it up and toss it in the garbage right behind the birth certificate and the first postcard and go back to believing that there was nothing extraordinary about her life. She wished she had never known Jane O'Leary.

Riley didn't know how long she stood there, staring, examining the note. There were no identifying marks on it, nothing else except the ominous message. She looked up, hoping that someone would take credit, would tell her it was a joke. She waited for Shelby to pop out from somewhere, laughing.

But Riley was alone.

A couple kids had moved to the benches across the lot to wait for their rides. Someone was smoking out against the back forty, the curls of cigarette smoke catching on the overhead lights.

Riley's heart started to thud.

Numbly, she dug into her purse, this time refusing to look

down. Her eyes scanned the parking lot until her fingers closed around her phone.

"Riley!"

Riley whirled, the phone sliding out of her hand and skittering across the concrete. Someone was parked in the darkness.

And now that someone was running toward her.

Adrenaline poured through her, and every synapse was on high alert: *move-run-stop-scream.* Her chest tightened and everything about the weekend—every dead-end search, every time she saw the strange man in her peripheral vision—came crashing back over her, and Riley willed her legs to move, to turn, to run, but they wouldn't. Her mind splintered, telling her to go for the phone, to turn around and run.

"Riley!"

The man was coming closer. She tried to make him out, but the night fuzzed out anything recognizable.

"Who's there?" She was surprised by her own voice.

"Aw, turnip!"

Her dad popped over the curb and gathered her into a tight hug, completely oblivious to Riley's terror.

"Geez! I can feel your heart practically popping into my chest!" he said jovially.

"That's because you scared me half to death!" Riley snapped. "What are you doing here?"

"Mama Webber called Mama Spencer and let her know that Cassia was in labor and that Shelby was going to stay with the girls, so here I am."

Riley followed her father to the car, tossing her backpack over the front seat and settling in. She blew out a breath, hoping to stave off a heart attack as everything churned inside her head: who sent her the note? Was this her real father? She stole a glance, examining her dad's profile.

Ask them, JD's voice echoed in her head. *Ask to see your birth certificate.*

As quickly as the thought appeared, it was stamped out by another, more pressing one: *leave it alone.* Riley got into the car, slamming the door behind her.

Her teeth had barely stopped chattering, and she refused to look into her purse, knowing the postcard was there. She couldn't bring herself to throw it away, and now she couldn't bring herself to touch it. Any connection to Jane O'Leary—or the mysterious postcards—would keep her tethered here, jumping at every breath.

Leave it alone.

"You're awfully quiet tonight, turnip."

"I'm just tired, that's all." Riley pressed her head against the cool window glass and closed her eyes, as much to trick herself that she was tired as to trick her father. But she felt every bump in the road, heard her father every time he took a deep breath or rumbled a few lines from whatever song was playing on the oldies station.

Through lowered lashes, Riley watched her father's hand as it reached across the console, settling on the stereo.

She knew those hands. The long, thin fingers, the half-moon of white on his nails. They wouldn't hurt her. They wouldn't hurt anyone else.

They wouldn't steal a child.

She sat up when her father turned into the opening of the Blackwood Hills Estates. Everything was manicured and tended to outside the gate, and big spotlights illuminated bunches of petunias and sweet alyssum as they flourished out of their spots and nipped at the edge of the grass. The grass was large and sprawling, so green it looked almost cartoonish and fake. But there was a man in a grey jumpsuit crouched behind a dribbling sprinkler. He had an ill-fitting trucker's hat with the words STAR LANDSCAPING printed on it, and he looked up as Riley's father's car passed through the gates.

"Isn't it weird to have a guy doing landscaping in the middle of the night?"

"It's not that late. And to his credit, the guy was out here when I left to get you too. Hard worker. Besides, the floodlights make it look like daytime out there."

• • •

Riley dropped the plug in her bathtub and nudged on the faucet. She gave it a moment before she sunk into the extra-hot suds. Thoughts of Jane Elizabeth pricked at her peripheral.

I will not think about her. I'm done with that, done with stupid "adventures."

But even when she pulled her iPad into the bathroom and turned her favorite playlist way up, her thoughts went back to Jane. And every time she closed her eyes, it was a slide show—the plain, boring images on the postcards, the ominous notes on the other side, and the face of the man, smiling down at her from the train platform.

• • •

"You know what? You never finish anything. I'm not going to let you be my Lamaze coach because halfway through, you'll wimp out and leave me there, half a baby coming out of my—"

"I get it, Shelbs."

Shelby held the folded certificate and waved it at Riley as if she'd never seen it before.

"I just—I'm done with it, Shelbs. I checked everything. There is no information on any of these people. I'm telling you, it came with the baby book."

"Right." Shelby pushed her yogurt away and smoothed the certificate on the table. "They totally use a real sticker seal and actual stamped baby feet to make those throwaway inserts. You think I haven't seen a thousand baby books? I swear my mom bought an eighty pack after my first brother was born."

Riley tossed her a look.

"I know, Ry, you're totally right. You exhausted all available search options. If only there were some other way." She stroked a long, imaginary chin beard. "Or someone we could ask. You know, like, maybe the people who hid the baby book? If only there were some way to contact them…"

"Fine, Shelby."

"You don't even have to mention Jane's birth certificate. Just ask them to show you yours. That's all I'm asking."

"That's it? You'll drop this whole thing if I show you my birth certificate?"

"Totally. That way I know that you have one and I won't be

under civic obligation to turn you in to the police. I'll totally drop the Jane thing. But the postcard…"

Riley felt her eyes widen. She hadn't told Shelby about the second one, and sitting with her now, Riley wasn't sure she wanted to. She wanted to pretend they were nothing, but *someone* sent them. Someone knew her—maybe better than she knew herself. The thought sent icy fingers of fear up Riley's neck and she shivered. "I'm going to toss my stuff," she said, standing.

"Hey."

"Hey." Riley looked up to see JD smiling at her. Her heart did a double pump, but it was because of Jane, not JD.

"So, you're at school today."

"Yeah, why wouldn't I be?"

JD pushed his hands in his back pockets. "I don't know. Thought maybe if you found out your parents had snatched you or that you were Jane O'Leary, some sort of super spy, you'd ditch this place." He was grinning, his tone light, but the comment weighed on her.

"No, I'm just plain old Riley Spencer, daughter of Glen and Nadine Spencer." She said it as much for her benefit as for his. "I'm giving up on Jane. It was stupid anyway."

JD shrugged. "I thought it was kind of cool—trying to track down this mysterious girl."

Riley felt herself smile. "It was until I came to a hundred dead ends."

JD cocked an eyebrow. "Well, what mystery chick would let herself be found the first time someone goes looking for her?"

• • •

Riley was shoving her Spanish book into her backpack when Shelby approached her.

"Need a ride, toots?"

Riley shook her head. "My dad is picking me up on his way home from work."

"You know what you have to do tonight, right?"

"Um, conjugate irregular verbs until my eyes bleed?"

Shelby let out an exasperated groan. "No, you're going to get your birth certificate."

"Right."

"That's all I ask."

"Fine, Shelbs, whatever. Bye."

Shelby took a few steps backward and waved. "Good-bye, mysterious stranger."

Riley hiked up her backpack and grumbled. So she would ask her parents to see her birth certificate. They would show it to her. And Riley would know that *she* wasn't adopted or kidnapped. She would know that she wasn't Jane Elizabeth O'Leary.

But who was the real Jane Elizabeth?

"Hey, Riley!" Trevor Gallagher was making a beeline toward her.

Riley waved. "Hey, Trevor. What's up?"

"Just wanted to make sure you got the card."

The hairs on Riley's arms stood upright. "The card?"

"I put it on your purse after the carnival. Just wanted to make sure you got yours."

Riley nodded, dumbfounded, even as Trevor walked away.

Trevor Gallagher gave her the postcards? But why?

By the time Riley snapped back to reality, Trevor had been swallowed into the crowd of Hawthorne High students on their way out, and Riley couldn't find him.

"Hey, turnip!"

Riley spun to find her father leaning out the driver's side window.

"Oh, hey, Dad."

"Well, are you going to stand out there or get in the car?"

"I'm coming, sorry."

She closed the door behind her and her father hit the gas. But her mind was still processing Trevor and the postcards. She vowed to ask Trevor about them tomorrow.

"One mystery solved," she muttered under her breath.

"What's that, hon?"

"Nothing. Sorry."

They were just approaching the Blackwood Hills highway by the time the general post-school catch-up—*How was school? Do you have homework?*—was finished. Riley was quiet for a bit. She had filed away Trevor and the postcards—now it was time to appease her best friend.

Riley played with the seat belt crossing her chest. "So, I was thinking about taking driver's ed next semester."

She could see her father's cheeks push up into a grin. "And here I thought you weren't interested in getting your license."

"Well, I wasn't because I had Shelby, but now that we live all the way out here…" Riley swallowed. "So, you think it's a good idea?"

"Of course."

"The thing is, I need to bring my birth certificate to register." Riley cut her eyes to her father, working hard to track his every movement.

"You know, we've still got a lot of unpacking to do. I'm not even sure I know where your mother has your birth certificate, turnip. Maybe you'd better wait on the driving stuff until we're all settled."

Tears pricked at the back of Riley's eyes.

"No, I want to take it next semester. And wouldn't Mom have all our important records in a safe deposit box or something? Since we lost all our pictures and stuff at the other house."

Riley thought she saw a look of relief skitter over her father's face. "That old place! Do you remember that house? We had the most beautiful hydrangeas."

"I kind of remember. Why were all my baby pictures ruined again?"

"The roof leaked."

Riley worried her bottom lip. "But my birth certificate was fine. I'll bet Mom knows exactly where it is."

Riley watched her father nod slowly and swallow, his Adam's apple bobbing in his throat. "Sure. But you know that you won't be able to drive much next semester. Your mother and I both need our cars. She'll be off for summer when you are, so then you would be able to get a lot of practice time in. Take driver's education then and concentrate on school in between."

"But I can get my birth certificate, right? So I can be prepared?"

"No need to jump the gun, turnip. Mom and I can take care of it."

He turned and grinned at her, but Riley felt like she had been punched in the stomach.

• • •

Riley lay in her bed, staring up at the ceiling. The glint from the streetlight outside cut a yellow diagonal stripe from end to end that shifted with every howling screech of the wind.

She wasn't going to fall asleep.

Her mind was a constant churn of the past days' events, but tonight it always came back to the same thing: the postcards. She knew how Trevor had gotten the first one in her purse—it must have fallen in when Shelby grabbed the bag—but what about the next one?

I KNOW WHO YOU ARE.

He hadn't been on the college tour and the two didn't have any classes together this year. They were just casual friends—so casual Riley didn't even have his phone number or email address. Why send someone you hardly know postcards with weird, creepy messages?

Riley kicked off her covers and sat on the floor, pulling her purse into her lap. She yanked out everything—whatever she needed always seemed to migrate to the bottom—and pulled the postcards out of the depths. Only now, there was something wedged in between them.

Riley shook out a tiny envelope, her heart thundering in her throat. Another weird message? A note from Trevor explaining the cards?

Her name was written on the front of the envelope in blue ballpoint pen and underlined twice. She popped the envelope open and a gift card to Sweet Retreat fell out.

"Riley Spencer" was written in the "TO" portion; "FROM" was "The ASB."

She read:

> Thank you for volunteering for the HHS Winter Carnival. Enjoy
> a free ice cream cone courtesy of Sweet Retreat Ice Cream. The
> Associated Student Body.

Riley started to breathe hard. *That's* the card that Trevor was talking about when he asked if she had "gotten hers." He didn't know anything about the postcards.

He wasn't the one who dropped them into her purse.

SOMETHING LOST HAS NOW BEEN FOUND.

Riley felt a tightening in her chest as sweat pricked at her hairline. She felt the familiar pins and needles feeling in her hands and feet. She was starting to panic.

Outside, the wind cut a wild path, and within seconds, the rain started like a snare drum, an insistent rhythm against the window. Her curtains caught and fluttered up, and Riley went to the window, slamming the one-inch open section closed.

A good gust of wind…

The hairs on the back of Riley's neck stood up, pricking electricity into her skin. Someone had come into her house. Someone had pulled the webpage of a missing child up on her computer and walked out of the house, leaving the front door open.

Someone who knew who she was.

• • •

The house was deathly quiet when Riley woke up the next morning. When she padded down the stairs, hers was the only place setting on the table—the usual bowl-plate-spoon, a glass of juice, and the little white pill. She hadn't had any reaction since she stopped taking it. She hadn't felt better or worse. She didn't want to believe that maybe her parents were drugging her, shoving pills down her throat that might make her forget things or make her more compliant, or whatever they did. She rolled the pill between her forefinger and thumb before dropping it into the sink and flipping on the garbage disposal. The gurgling, chopping sound of the blades felt like they were eating their way through Riley's life, her normalcy. Everything was a chopped-up mess.

There was a note propped against her juice glass:

We're at the farmers' market. Eat breakfast!

There were the usual *x*'s and *o*'s, and her mom's flowery signature on the bottom.

Riley put her unused bowl and spoon away, her stomach turning in on itself, anxiety and uncertainty turning her saliva sour.

She nearly dropped her juice glass when her cell phone started blaring.

"Hey, Shelbs. You totally made me jump."

"That's because you're living in the neighborhood that technology forgot. I'm picking you up. I need a Cinnabon and a new backpack. One of the twins barfed in mine."

"Gross. But my parents aren't here. I can't leave."

Shelby groaned into the phone. "Call them. Tell them I'll pick you up and make you wear a seat belt and take your Flintstone vitamins. Seriously. It's a matter of puke or death."

Riley sucked in a breath, one that bolstered the nagging suspicion in her gut. "You know what? Head over. I'll be waiting outside for you."

Riley shimmied into her jacket and hiked up her purse before settling on the porch steps. The sky was a bright, crisp blue, all evidence of last night's pounding rain gone. The sunshine bounced off the windows, giving the impression that the half-empty Blackwood Hills Estates was a cheery, bustling neighborhood.

Riley shivered. Her cell phone chirped.

TWIN BARFERS R TWIN BARFING. C U IN 20.

She looked at the locked door behind her then speed-walked to the empty house across the street. If someone was peering into her window, or even just staring her down the night she left for the school trip, she wanted to know who they were.

She knocked and waited, pressing her ear against the door.

Silence. She found the doorbell and mashed that too, the same chimes as her house had making a muffled ring inside. Riley was peering into the first-floor windows, her eyes scanning the empty foyer, the desolate living room, when she heard a twig crack behind her.

She stiffened immediately.

"Are you moving in or something?"

Riley whirled. A girl was standing on the stretch of dirt that should have been landscaping, her hands on her hips. She looked to be about Riley's age.

"Uh, no. I just thought that maybe someone lived here."

The girl swung her head. "Not likely. My parents just looked at the place. There's a big gaping hole in one of the windows. Someone was squatting there. The real estate lady was super embarrassed." The girl grinned. "She ran in front of us and dumped all his shit in the trash."

Riley's skin started tingling. Someone had been watching her. It was true.

"Hey, Bryn!"

Riley looked over the girl's shoulder to see a couple standing outside of a car, waving.

"That's my parents," Bryn said. "Maybe I'll see you around."

Riley stared after the girl as her stomach started to roil. Someone was squatting there. Someone was watching her. She edged around the front and tugged at the garbage bag on the curb, yanking until it tore open. A tattered blanket fell out, a crunched up sweatshirt that looked like it had been used for a pillow. A couple of Big Gulp cups and Snicker's bar wrappers and, shoved way in the back, a cheap pair of binoculars. Riley reached for them, her entire body feeling slimy when her hand closed over them. She pulled them out and the case came with them, a Big Mac wrapper stuck to the side.

"Gross."

Something rattled as she went to toss the binoculars back. There was something in the case. Riley rooted around until her fingers closed around the tiny metal charm. It looked like a silver angel—or it would have, if its wing and head hadn't been broken off. She studied it until Shelby's beast-mobile coughed up the street. Then she jammed it in her pocket.

"You look like you've seen a ghost. Or your parents having sex," Shelby said when Riley belted herself into her seat.

"I think someone has been watching me," Riley said, turning down the radio. She jabbed a finger toward the house. "From there."

"Like a new neighbor? Is he hot? Please say he's hot."

Riley shook her head. "I'm not even completely sure it's a guy. I couldn't see anything. This is getting creepy. I think a guy was following me in Granite Cay too."

"You think, or you know?"

"What's that supposed to mean?"

Shelby flipped on her blinker, gunning the old car onto the highway. "It means you tend to lean toward the paranoid."

"*I* do? You're the one who's sure I've been kidnapped."

"And that turned out to be nothing, right? What did your parents say?"

Riley bit her thumbnail. "I didn't ask them about Jane."

"Let me get this straight: you jump on a train with a total delinquent to go searching for a girl on a birth certificate, and when that turns up zilch, you don't even bother to ask your parents. James Bond you are not."

Riley stared out the windshield, pressing her feet firmly against the floor. She needed something solid; she needed something to connect to.

"They wouldn't let me see my birth certificate."

"What?"

Riley swallowed. "They said it was in a box somewhere and they would 'take care of it.' My mom told me all my baby stuff was ruined in a flood, but my dad told me it was a leaky roof. My mom gives me pills every morning, but I can't even look at the bottle."

"There has to be logical explanations for all that, Ry. I was totally messing with you. I didn't think you'd take it so seriously."

Riley sucked in a breath. "There's something else. I was at home the other night and the doorbell rang. When I came back upstairs, there was a poster of a missing kid on my screen."

"Who was at the door? Who was the kid?" Shelby rolled to a stop and gaped at Riley. "My God, I didn't think it was actually true. Was the missing kid you?"

"No one was at the door. I don't know who the baby was." She reached into her purse and handed Shelby the second postcard. "And then there was this."

"*I know who you are*," Shelby read out loud. Her cheeks paled. "Ry, this is serious. You have to talk to your parents. Or go to the police or something."

"I can't go to the police. What if they arrest my parents? And I don't know if I can talk to my parents. What do I say? 'Did you snatch me off the street?'"

"Who sent you this?"

Riley swung her head. "I don't know. It's the same person who sent the other one, I guess. I mean, obviously. How many people send random, one-line postcards to strangers?"

"Whoever sent them is no stranger, Ry. *I know who you are…*"

They drove the rest of the way to the mall in silence, Riley's phone ringing as they stepped into the first store.

"Hey, Mom."

"Where are you?"

Riley sighed. "I'm at the mall with Shelby."

"No one gave you permission to leave the house. You didn't even call us or leave a note."

She felt the heat flicker in the pit of her stomach. "I'm not a little kid, Mom. Shelby just picked me up and we're at the mall. No big deal."

Her mother spat something back but Riley's eye was wandering, caught on a little girl and her mother. They were holding hands but when the kid—five or six years old at best—caught sight of the play structure in the middle of the mall, she dropped her mother's hand and took off running.

Maybe I just ran away, and my parents picked me up?

"Do you hear me, Riley? Tell Shelby to bring you home right now."

Riley watched the scene in front of her. The mother of the little girl was immediately panic-stricken, her whole face crumpling in the seconds that her daughter disappeared then reappeared on the play structure. The mother had a hand splayed on her chest as if to stop her thundering heart.

Riley tore her eyes away.

"I'm not going to make her drive me all the way home. We just got here."

"Then your father and I will meet you in front of the coffee-house in twenty minutes."

Shelby came out of the store, brows raised. "What's up?"

"The wardens are picking me up in twenty."

"Seriously?" Shelby's face fell.

"Yeah. But you go find your barf-free backpack. I better do as I was told and tether myself to the coffee place."

"Use your one jailhouse phone call to call me."

The mall was getting crowded, and Riley wound herself through clutches of singles and groups when she felt fingertips brush against her bare arm. There was a man beside her, staring straight ahead. He was older, maybe in his twenties, and stood a head taller.

She saw the man's lips move, thought she heard him mutter, "Don't worry."

"Excuse me?"

He didn't repeat himself, but Riley's eyes followed his fingers as they tightened around her wrist. Her heart was slamming into her ribcage, her pulse hammering underneath his thumb.

"I'll scream," Riley said. "If you don't let me go right now, I'll scream."

His grip tightened, every finger like a steel band digging in. "Don't do that."

Her mind was racing. All around her people swarmed, chatting, shopping, moving right past without even looking at her. Their chatter was overwhelming. Even if she could scream, she didn't think anyone would hear her.

"There are police," she said, "right after the next shop. Let me go and I won't say anything, I promise." Her lower lip started to tremble, her eyes filling with tears—but she gritted her teeth. She wouldn't let this man see her cry. "The police—"

The man gripping her arm gave Riley a quick glance—just quick enough for her to memorize his thick jaw, his ice-blue eyes, and the scar that cleaved his lower lip. "You won't scream and you won't say anything to the police. You wouldn't do that to your parents."

Riley stopped walking, everything inside of her running cold.

"How do you know my parents?"

He tugged her arm. "Keep walking."

Heat, picking up speed as it sped through her veins, was breaking out all over her. There was a tightening in her chest.

"Who are you?"

A muscle flicked along the man's jawline but he didn't immediately say anything.

"Let me go right now." Her voice sounded breathy, desperate.

"Hear me out. Trust me. We're in a public place, Riley. I'm not going to hurt you."

"H—how do you know my name?"

He didn't answer or loosen his grip, and Riley fumbled, walking along. "Why should I believe you?"

"Because your parents aren't who they say they are."

Riley's whole body went rigid. "What?"

"They're lying to you. They're lying to everybody. Your name is Jane O'Leary."

She couldn't help but stop and look up. "Jane?"

"My name is Tim. Have your parents told you anything about me? Have they told you anything about the O'Learys?"

"N-no."

"They won't tell you the truth. They'll tell you something crazy; they'll tell you that they're trying to protect you, but they're not. They're bad people, Jane."

Riley ripped Tim's hands from her arm. "You're crazy. You don't know what you're talking about. My parents aren't bad." She could feel the tears rimming her eyes but she gritted her teeth, refusing to cry.

"They're going to isolate you. They won't let you talk to anyone."

The heavy iron gates of the Blackwood Hills Estates flashed in Riley's mind. So did her father, scrutinizing her cell phone bill. *That's normal*, Riley told herself. *I'm seventeen, not a prisoner.*

"Why should I believe anything you say anyway?"

Tim turned to face her, his eyes a slicing crystal blue. "Because I'm your brother."

The breath was snatched out of Riley's lungs.

"Come with me."

She fumbled backward. "No."

His hand was on her arm again. "Come on, Jane. You're not safe here. If they even know that you've seen me, they'll hurt you. They'll hurt us both."

Riley's heart was pulsing in her ears. Her skin suddenly felt too small, too tight. *I don't believe you,* she wanted to scream. *I don't believe a goddamn word you're saying.* But she couldn't force her lips to move.

Tim was digging in his pocket, his eyes scanning the crowd before them. Riley's breath hitched.

He's crazy and he's going to shoot me now. He's going to stab me, to set off a bomb. That's what crazy people do. Crazy people who claim they're my brother.

Instead, he pressed a card into her hand. "Call me. I will come and get you from wherever you are." His eyes cut back to the crowd. "They're dangerous, Jane. Don't say a single word or they'll disappear again." He shifted his gaze back to her. "You'll disappear."

The coffeehouse was directly in front of them, and Riley found herself begging for her parents while pleading that they shouldn't come. If this man was going to kill her, she didn't want her parents to get hurt. But she desperately wanted them to save her.

The door opened as if on cue, and Riley's parents stepped into the store.

Tim saw them too.

She gasped, sucking in air like it was her last breath and rooting her feet to the ground.

"Come on." He tugged her arm at the same moment Riley's

father caught her eye. Suddenly, it was as if the whole mall was staring, and there was a cool spot on her wrist where Tim's hand had been.

SEVEN

Riley stared out the window the whole ride home. Her parents were taking turns lecturing and grounding her, but all she could think about was the man—Tim—his fingers gripping her wrist, and his voice: *Your parents are lying to you.*

She glanced up and stared at the backs of their heads, catching first her father's reflection in the rearview mirror and then her mother's.

Not my *parents.*

Riley shifted in her seat, feeling the heat of panic as it inched in. *What happens now?* The man said she wouldn't call the police because she "wouldn't do that" to her parents.

Do what?

Riley swallowed and clamped her mouth shut. Her stomach was in her throat, and she was certain that if she opened her mouth, she would vomit.

This can't be happening…I don't have a brother. I can't believe I'm even considering what this guy is saying.

But he knew her name. And he knew Jane.

I'm Jane Elizabeth O'Leary?

No.

My parents aren't liars. I just want this all to go away.

They pulled through the neighborhood gates and Riley glanced down at her phone. There was a text from JD.

FOUND SOMETHING.

Riley's breath caught. Her fingers were flying over the keyboard when her mother leaned into the backseat, her hand closing over the phone.

"We said no phone, Ry."

Riley looked up, stunned as her mother slipped the phone into her purse.

"You can't do that!"

"And you can't just take off whenever you want to." Her father cut the engine and stepped out of the car.

Riley was about to respond, but he looked over his shoulder at her, his glare so severe that it gave her the chills.

"Go to your room."

Riley silently climbed the stairs then immediately turned on her laptop, tagging JD for a chat.

SMILYRILY: Whatd u find out?

HNTR41: Hi to u too

SMILYRILY: Sry. Hi. Parents took my phone.

HNTR41: Sux. Was doing some research on ur Jane.

SMILYRILY: AND?????

HNTR41: Wait. Downloading the pic u sent.

SMILYRILY: I didn't send you anything. What did you find out???

HNTR41: Do you know if Jane had a brother Tim?

SMILYRILY: OMG I met Tim today. He grabbed my arm.

Riley sat back from the screen, wondering how much to tell JD. And even if she told him the truth—the truth as it happened—what could she say? The computer chirped when JD messaged her back.

HNTR41: Holy crap, R! That's creepy. How did u do that?

SMILYRILY: Wait—Do what???

A photo icon popped up on her screen.

HNTR41: U sent this.

Riley clicked on the icon and watched it bounce as a picture loaded, the image filling the whole screen. There was a glowing laptop in the center and a pair of hands resting on the keys. They were female hands and she immediately recognized the Panic Purple nail polish—because she was wearing it too. The head that was blocking the screen was familiar as well. Even in silhouette, she could see the tendrils that were falling out of the back of her ponytail.

"Oh my God!"

Riley jumped back from her screen and turned, clawing at her wall for the device that was filming her—there had to be one. But her walls were smooth, completely unmarred.

She yanked open the bathroom and closet doors, half hoping that her phantom photographer would be inside, half begging that he was long gone. The tears were burning tracks over her cheeks, and every step that Riley took she was sure that someone was tracking, watching, listening to her every breath.

When she heard a car door slam, Riley's mind started spinning, and she was taking the stairs two at a time. She heard her parents yelling at her but was too focused to make out the words. She flung open the front door and was hit with a cold rush of night air then the burning of something tightening against her throat, pulling her backward. Her father had a handful of her T-shirt.

"Riley, stop!"

"Dad, Dad, there's someone out there! There's someone outside, they—they took a picture and—"

"Riley! Stop. Breathe."

She whipped her head toward the street and then back to her father. "There was…" Riley's words drifted off.

There was no one in the street. It was dark—not ominous, just regular nighttime dark—with a crushing wind that made skeletal leaves cartwheel past.

"What are you talking about?"

Riley tried to pull in a deep breath, but it was like trying to breathe through a straw. She pressed her hand to her chest and blinked away the tears that rimmed her eyes.

"Breathe, Riley. One, two…" Her mother was speaking to her now, her hands on Riley's arms, slate-gray eyes focused on her daughter.

Riley tried to do as her mother said. She felt a bead of sweat start at her hairline and make its way down the side of her face.

"Maybe we should call Dr. Morley and have him check your antianxiety medication. Maybe your body is getting used to it?" Her mother's eyebrows were knitted with worry, and Riley pinched her eyes shut.

Antianxiety, she breathed. *My parents aren't trying to drug me.*

After what seemed like a lifetime, she was finally able to take in a full breath.

"What happened, Riley?" her mother asked gently.

Riley looked from her mother to her father then out to the darkness on the street. "I thought I saw someone outside. Someone watching me."

Her parents shared a look. "Like a Peeping Tom?"

"No." Riley shrugged out of her mother's arms. "Someone driving by. Or in a car, stopped. Just like—I was instant messaging—"

"Instant messaging? You're grounded, remember?"

"Yeah, but I—"

"Your father and I were very clear, Riley."

"But, Mom, it was just a—I was just talking to a friend and then—"

Riley watched her father suck in a deep breath. He knitted his brow and set his lips, and her stomach dropped. Riley knew that look; she *loathed* that look.

"Go up to your room."

"Dad—"

"You want to make your punishment worse? Up to your room."

"Someone was watching—"

"There was no one outside, Riley. Your father and I were here the whole time."

"Trust me, if someone has their eye on us—on you—we'd know about it. Now up to your room before I get unreasonable," her father said.

Riley opened her mouth and then closed it, looking at the hard expressions on her parents' faces. She knew that if she said anything—if she protested or confessed—her parents would dismiss her. They weren't going to listen to anything she had to say.

She trudged up the stairs, her heart a stomach-dropping thud each time her foot fell. She didn't want to be in her room. She didn't want to be locked into a box where someone—somehow—had photographed her.

Riley swallowed at the lump in her throat as she reached out to turn the doorknob. She flung open her bedroom door and finally let out the breath she didn't know she was holding. She scanned the room with wide eyes before tiptoeing across the carpet and snatching up her laptop. Her parents had commanded her to her room—she was willing to compromise. Riley slid down in the doorway and pulled her computer onto her lap.

She went back to her screen and blinked at the message now displayed.

"'Internet connection lost'? What the hell?"

She typed in her password, groaning when nothing happened. She typed in the WEP key and the server password. The computer dinged and red letters lined the screen: SMILYRILY NO LONGER HAS ACCESS TO THIS ACCOUNT.

• • •

Riley's eyes were bloodshot and raw the following morning. She had spent the night turning, considering: the open front door that she knew she had locked. The postcard, the photograph—Tim. She shuddered. Something about him—about the way he said her name, the way he looked down at her and said *she* was Jane—it struck something cold and dark way down in Riley's belly. Not fear, exactly.

Something much, much worse.

She thought of the hard look in her father's eyes as he yanked her into the house.

Did her parents know that she had met Tim?

"Stop it, Ry," she muttered.

"They're going to try to isolate you…"

The severe red letters barring Riley from her email account flashed in her mind.

She had had her phone and Internet taken once before, but that was after she *failed* a midterm—not after an impromptu trip to the mall.

I KNOW WHO YOU ARE…

Was the note from Tim?

The thought stabbed at her heart, and guilt washed over her. Would she really believe a stranger, someone who approached her in a mall, more than she believed her own parents?

Her eyes instantly went to her laptop and the folded-up birth certificate hidden underneath. She wanted to snatch it up and tear it into a thousand tiny pieces. If she could tear it small enough, make it disappear, then maybe everything would go back to normal and she wouldn't be Jane Elizabeth O'Leary.

"I'm not her," Riley said defiantly, as if somehow Tim could hear her. "I'm not Jane O'Leary."

Even with her admission, she knew that she was beyond the ability to stamp out errant thoughts about Jane. Even when she focused on the hot water pouring over her head in the shower, Jane was there, whispering, wondering about Riley.

No baby pictures…the nightmares…

Riley had been plagued with nightmares for as long as she could remember. They were always the same. They always chilled her to her very core, leaving her skittish and cold for hours after she woke.

Maybe I'm remembering something…maybe it was the night Jane—I?—went missing…

She turned off the shower and dressed, not bothering to flick on the radio like she usually did. She didn't even dry her hair, opting instead to weave the wet strands into some semblance of a bun. She picked her way down the stairs as if she were a stranger in her own house, averting her eyes at the memory wall her mother had finished—pictures of Riley and her parents at a park, at Disneyland, a three-year-old Riley hugging Mickey Mouse, her eyes the size of saucers.

Nothing before three years old, that same suspicious voice in her head breathed. *Because Riley Alan Spencer didn't exist before that?*

She shook off the thought and walked into the kitchen where

her father glanced up at her over the edge of his newspaper. Her mother was scrubbing something more intently than she needed to, and Riley pulled a chair from the table, sitting down silently. Her mother had left her a bowl and a spoon, her pill and her juice, and now she turned, setting the "end of" cereal container in front of Riley. It was Riley's favorite—a big plastic container that contained all the leftovers of cereal boxes when there wasn't enough for a respectable bowl. Everything got shoved in there willy-nilly, and Riley loved the surprise, loved the taste of sweet-crunchy-healthy-marshmallow packed into every bite.

But now it made her stomach roil.

Her mother sat down wordlessly and poked a knife into a grapefruit half while Riley chewed her cereal, biting down until it was paste, her jaws aching after four bites. She glanced at her father, who snapped his newspaper and turned the page. She could see her mother in her peripheral sight, hear the sound of the serrated knife sawing through grapefruit flesh. She could hear the pulse of her own heart, throbbing in her ears. Everyone was so deathly silent, but the silence was so deafeningly loud. Riley reached into her pocket and fingered the edge of the birth certificate. On a whim, she had pulled it from under her laptop and stashed it there. She set her spoon down.

"Why are there no pictures of me from before I was a toddler?"

Her mother looked up, her eyelashes fluttering as though she were stunned. "What do you mean, Riley? You know about the flood."

Riley sucked her teeth, taking in a deep, slow breath. "Dad said the roof leaked."

She didn't bother to look up, but Riley knew her father did. She heard his newspaper as he laid it on the table.

"What's this about, Riley?"

"Before we moved to the house on Kemper, where did we live?"

Her mother laughed, and Riley couldn't help dissecting it—a guilty laugh, trying in vain to cover up her nerves? A standard giggle because Riley had asked the question before? She didn't want to examine her parents the way she was, but everything inside her told her that something was wrong.

Her father carefully set his hands on the table and leveled his gaze at Riley. "Before we moved to Crescent City, we lived in Chicago. Do you remember the tiny apartment there?"

"Tiny?" her mother giggled. "Do you remember, before we brought Riley home, how big we thought that place was?"

Riley's head snapped up. "Brought me home from where?"

Her mother's stare was steady, her lips held in a thin line. "From the hospital, honey. You were too young to remember—you probably don't remember that little place at all. We left when you were—"

"We left when I was three, because the roof leaked," Riley finished. "And then what?"

"Well," her father cut in, "we left that place as fast as our little legs could carry us. The roof almost came in—in winter in Chicago! You have no idea how cold the weather can actually get. You've been way too spoiled by the weather out here."

He smiled jovially at Riley, but every part of her was tense, focusing.

Riley's mother stepped in. "We moved in with one of your

father's colleagues for a short time while we looked for a place of our own—big enough for all three of us. And then your father got the offer out here. Oh, we were so relieved. Your dad would get to run his own store."

Riley blinked at her mother, feeling her own mouth tighten as disbelief set in. "And my grandparents?"

"Your grandparents passed away. Mom's parents and my mother before you were born, and my father when you were much too small to remember." He spoke slowly as if trying to make sure that Riley understood, could make the connections—or as though he were speaking from a script, carefully trying to make sure every line was right.

Riley felt herself bristle, and her father slipped back into that easy, relaxed smile.

"Riley, why are you all of a sudden so interested in all of this? You know all of it. You were born in Chicago. We moved to California when you were about three—" Her father started to recount everything they had just said while a flicker of interest turned into a white-hot fire in Riley. Her blood was pulsing as if every lie her parents told her—everything so carefully rehearsed—thrummed under Riley's skin.

"It's not true," Riley said to her cereal bowl.

"What's that, hon?"

Riley swallowed, earnestly trying to keep her heart from slamming against her ribcage. She felt faint. Her skin felt tight and hot. She tried to steady her breath as much as possible.

"Who's Jane Elizabeth O'Leary?"

The sentence was out before Riley knew she'd said it. It hung out there in the air between her parents and herself, an untouched thing with a heft and a weight, a life all its own.

The room was deathly silent.

Riley's heart clanged like a fire bell.

Her father's eyebrows shot up. Her mother's hands fluttered over the grapefruit knife, leaving it stabbed in a center section. She clasped both hands together, folding them into her lap. The silence could have gone on for five seconds or five hours—Riley had no idea. All she could see was her parents' eyes on her, their breaths coming in tight little wisps.

"Were you going through your father and my things? You know you are not supposed to go through our things without asking."

"I found her birth certificate by mistake."

Her mother took a slow, metered breath as if she were counting to ten, trying to pull herself together.

"By mistake?"

"It was in my baby book."

"Which I know is in my closet, which I know I didn't give you permission to rifle through." Her mother worked to keep her voice even and steady, but Riley could detect a slight tremble in it.

"OK, I'm sorry. But the birth certificate was in *my* baby book. Don't I have the right to look through my own baby book? It's about my life." Riley licked her bottom lip, suddenly completely unsure. "Isn't it?"

Her father picked up his newspaper, his eyes flicking from Riley back to it as he folded the paper into a perfect rectangle.

He touched Riley's mother's hand and they exchanged a look that Riley couldn't recognize.

"Nadine, Riley has every right to see her baby book."

"I don't care about the baby book," Riley said, louder than she intended. "I want to know about the birth certificate. This birth certificate." She slapped the paper on the table and felt like she was being punched in the stomach when she saw her mother's eyes go to it and immediately start to tear up.

"Glen," she whispered.

"Riley," her father started, "this birth certificate is not important. You don't need to bother with Jane Elizabeth." He reached out and began to slide the birth certificate toward him.

Riley's arm shot out like a cobra attacking. She smacked her palm on the table, on the birth certificate, stopping her father, surprising even herself.

"Who is she?"

Her father swung his head. "Riley, just trust us. It's nothing you need to bother with."

"Then why won't you tell me?" she exploded. "If it's nothing, if it's just some birth certificate you found, why won't you tell me?" Her heart hammered and leapt into her throat as she locked eyes with first her mother then her father. "Is it because it's mine?"

She hadn't meant to say the last part but it was there now, out. A sob choked in Riley's throat.

"Did you kidnap me?"

EIGHT

The silence was palpable, and Riley's mind was racing. *What will happen now? Will they admit it? Will I be reunited with my "real" parents? Will these parents go to prison?*

She didn't want that. She didn't want a new family; she didn't want to live with anyone else.

Riley's heart started to thud. Her father ran a printing store. He helped giddy brides pick out wedding invitations and donated a banner to the Crescent City Little League team every year. She couldn't imagine him caged, like an animal, with all those criminals.

But if he kidnapped me, he is *a criminal.*

She thought about her mother, now sitting primly at the table. She was an elementary school nurse who wore horrible, holiday-themed turtlenecks underneath her sterile white smock. She had a whole drawer stocked with Sponge Bob and princess-themed Band-Aids. She got cards and drawings from the kids at the school and tacked them up on the fridge, right next to Riley's stuff.

Not criminals…

"Oh, Riley," her mother said finally, breaking the silence. "Honey."

Riley began to shake her head, fear like she had never felt crashing through her body, making her break out in a cold sweat.

"Did I have a family? Are they looking for me? Did they ever come looking for me?"

Her mother started to shake her head and her father opened his mouth as if to say something, but shut it. Instead, he looked to his wife, to the tears flowing down her cheeks.

Riley's palms were wet. Her stomach folded in on itself.

I just accused my parents of kidnapping.

And her mother was—laughing?

Riley swung her head, incredulous. Tears flowed over her mother's cheeks, landing with tiny little thuds on her bare plate. But her shoulders shook, and she was pressing her hand against her open mouth, trying to stifle the giggles.

"No, Riley," her father said, resting his hand on her mom's shoulder, "we didn't kidnap you. You're our daughter. We're your parents."

Relief washed over Riley and suddenly she felt light, silly. "I'm sorry," she said, looking at her hands. "It's just that I couldn't find any information about the baby and the parents and—who does it belong to, anyway? Who's Jane?"

Her mother immediately stopped laughing and her father's eyes went wide. "Did you ask anyone about Jane?"

"Well, no. I mean, I—"

"Riley, this is very important. Did you talk to anyone about Jane? Or about the O'Leary's?"

Riley's nerves kicked up again. "Well, Shelby was with me when I found the birth certificate." Riley bit her lip, considering. There was no reason to tell her parents about JD. No reason to tell them about her visit to the hospital or the hall of records. She shrugged, hoping it came off nonchalant. "That's it."

"How did you conduct your search?"

"What do you mean—?"

Her father hung his head, pressing his fingers against his temples. His tone was stern, impatient. "How, Riley?"

"Just on the Internet, geez. But I couldn't find Jane O'Leary. Who is she?"

Again, her parents exchanged a glance. This one was clearly stern, clearly questioning. Her father gave a short nod and pressed his chair away from the table, standing. "I'm going to call Mr. Hempstead," he said before leaving the kitchen.

"Mom, what is Dad—?"

Her mother put her hand on Riley's shoulder and turned her chair to face her. "Ry, you are Jane Elizabeth O'Leary."

Someone sucked all the air out of the room. Riley wanted to cry, to scream, to question, but all she could do was sit there, stone-faced, staring at her mother. After what seemed like hours, she was able to get her lips to move.

"My parents?"

"We're your parents. We're the O'Learys."

It started low in her belly. A flicker, a flame. A fire. Riley tried to hold herself, hugging her arms across her chest. It was all so ridiculous. She started to giggle, just like her mother. A maniacal, loose, bobbing giggle that weakened her entire body, made it shake throughout.

"What do you mean, we're the O'Learys? We're the Spencers. I'm not Jane, I'm Riley."

Riley became very aware of her mother's hands on hers, gripping tighter. "It's not important, Riley. None of this is. You're our daughter, we're your parents. Forget all the rest of this."

"But—"

Riley's mother shook her head, batting at the air like her whole confession was an annoying gnat at her ear—nothing more. "Don't worry about it. Please, Riley, just trust us."

Riley yanked her hands free and sat back in her chair. "Trust you about what? You didn't tell me anything except that Jane Elizabeth is me. Why do I have a different name? Why do we all have different names and I have a fake birth certificate? Are you my birth parents? I don't understand."

Riley saw her father pacing in the next room, a cell phone pressed to his ear. He didn't look like a stranger. He looked like her father who was a goof and called her turnip and did horrible Jimmy Stewart impressions at Christmastime. She saw him mutter something into the phone and then he took it from his ear, pushing it into his back pocket. When he turned to face Riley, he was still her father but his face was ashen and worn, as though he had aged ten years in the walk from the kitchen to the den.

"Riley, you're going to be late for school." He picked up her backpack and held it out to her. Riley stared at it blankly.

"What? You tell me I'm—I'm a different person and—and I'm just supposed to go to school and act like nothing happened?"

Her father's eyes were flat and emotionless. His face was stern, but otherwise void of anything Riley could recognize. "You need to trust us, Riley."

Riley felt the tears stinging at the back of her eyes as she looked from her mother to her father.

She snatched her backpack. "I don't see what I am supposed to trust about you two. You haven't told me anything true. You haven't told me anything that makes any sense at all!" The tears were falling freely now, heat breaking over her cheeks. "'We have this fake birth certificate for you, but you should just trust us.' 'We've been lying to you your whole life, but you just have to trust us'?"

"Riley, we're still your parents—"

"Are you? How do I know that? Why would my own parents change my name and my birthday? Why would my own parents hide a birth certificate for a girl who doesn't exist?"

Her father grabbed her shoulder. Riley couldn't tell if she was hyper aware or if her father's grip was more severe that he meant. She saw his Adam's apple bob as he swallowed, saw the desperation in his eyes as they skimmed over her then went to his wife.

"Glen, she shouldn't go to school today. We should keep her here with us until Mr. Hempstead can get here."

"Why can't you just tell me right now? Why do we have to wait for some guy I don't even know?"

"Please, Riley. It'll be easier this way. Mr. Hempstead—"

"Forget it. I don't want to be here! I don't want to be here with people who are lying to me!"

Riley snatched her jacket and hiked up her backpack, clearing the kitchen in three long strides. She threw open the front door and pounded through it, slamming it with a tremendous snap behind her.

Hands fisted, tears rolling down her cheeks and sliding over her chin, Riley ran down the sidewalk, loving the lone echo of her sneakers as they hit the concrete. It was somehow soothing to know that the sound that reflected back was her own—even if she wasn't entirely sure who *she* was.

She heard the garage door opening somewhere behind her. The faint sound of car doors snapping shut, of an engine being revved.

Riley couldn't stand it.

She crossed behind a bank of nearly finished houses, skipping through backyards that hadn't been fenced yet, until she was up against the wrought iron bars of the Blackwood Hills Estates. She tossed her backpack over the top and shimmied through the bars, taking one last look over her shoulder. She saw her parents in their car, slowly driving away from the house, her mother scanning the sidewalks, her hands pressed against her cheeks. Riley waited for the familiar pang of guilt or sadness but got nothing. She just pressed her legs harder, face against the wind, and took off running.

It didn't take long for her breath to burn in her lungs and for Riley to meet up with the street. Her parents, had they gone toward the school, would have already passed her, so Riley walked along the road, backpack hiked up. She was huffing and out of breath, but her anger pushed her forward.

• • •

Riley spent the entire day curled on the closet floor of one of the model homes that lined the front of the Blackwood Hills Estates. When the fog swallowed the sun and turned the sky a smoky gray, she slipped out of the closet and into the street, unsure whether she was ready to face her parents.

She heard a car engine moving slowly up the street and her heartbeat mirrored her heavy footfalls. Her parents. They must have been out looking all day. But the car's engine revved and it sped past her, a black blur taking the curve in front of her house with a little too much speed. The screech of the wheels echoed and Riley rolled her eyes then sucked in a breath, steadying herself on her front porch.

The whole house was dark and she had to step into the meager yellow beam of streetlight as she searched for her keys.

"Damn," she muttered when she realized that they were lying on the kitchen table. She beelined back up the walk and pushed the doorbell, listening to the stupid chime as it echoed.

No one answered.

Riley tried the door and wasn't surprised to find it locked. She dumped her backpack and went to the backyard, yanking the sliding glass door and trying all the windows. She was locked out—keys inside, cell phone tucked in her father's desk drawer.

"Crap."

She was coming around the front again when she noticed the

black car parked across the street. It was a few houses down and with the headlights off, bled into the darkness.

Riley took a step, and the headlights flipped on. The gravel crunched under her sneakers, and the black car's engine came gurgling to life.

A cold sliver of fear raced up her spine, and her adrenaline started to rush.

She fisted her hands and started down the sidewalk, aiming toward the glowing lights of the realtor office and the cheery faux neighborhood of houses behind it. Riley's was one of the houses at the furthest end of the horseshoe-shaped development, so she walked with purpose, her heart hammering as she passed the bones of houses yet to be finished. She didn't need to turn to know the black car was following her.

As she sped up, it did too, the patter of its engine swallowing up the sounds of her sneakers pounding the pavement. She sidestepped into the dirt, cutting through a gravelly front yard and slipping into a new model that was half studs, half walls. She dipped behind a piece of wallboard, and the black car flipped on its high beams. Blinding white light flooded over the house.

Riley was certain the sound of her heart slamming against her ribcage would give her away as she huddled down. The sweat beaded on her upper lip, and her teeth were chattering. The wallboard stopped about three feet to her left, and the rest of the houses were an unhelpful forest of narrow two-by-fours. Behind her, the wrought iron gate penned her in.

She was trapped.

The car engine revved and then all at once, Riley was plunged back into darkness.

Riley let out the breath she didn't know she was holding. The engine had cut too, and while her eyes worked to adjust to the pitch black, her ears pricked, trying to pick some semblance of sound out of the silence.

And then she heard it. The car door opening. The sound of a boot digging into the gravel. She heard someone suck on a cigarette, smelled the faint tarry smell as it carried on the breeze.

The man ground out the cigarette and took another step.

Riley rolled to her hands and knees, but her muscles felt slack and heavy. She willed herself forward, cringing as bits of wood splintered into her clawing fingertips and the toes of her shoes shifted debris underneath her. Her breath was coming in quick, short bursts. Her heart was pounding. Everything she did was loud.

"Come out, come out," the man sang, his voice deep and eerie.

Riley crawled to another corner and quietly slipped off the house's foundation. She was lying on her back, pressing her body into the dirt, trying to blend into the dirt and new construction.

She refused to think what was wriggling underneath her.

"Riley?"

Her skin crawled when he said her name.

"I'm not going to hurt you. I just want to talk."

He took another hard step and the wood floor slab vibrated under his weight.

I have to get out of here, Riley thought. The tears were pouring from her eyes, rolling over her cheeks and wetting the earth on either side of her. *If I don't get out of here now, he's going to find me.*

"Come out, come out wherever you are…Jane."

NINE

Terror, like a heavy weight, set on Riley's chest.

"I need to talk about your parents, Glen and Nadine."

Riley's stomach turned over.

Now. Nownownownownow.

She shifted in the dirt, clenching her eyes shut when a pebble rolled away from her foot. The man stopped laughing, and Riley lunged forward, vaulting across the front yard and onto the sidewalk. She ran hard, her feet aching, her thighs burning. She kept her eye focused on the first house on the block, the one with glowing lights and a car parked in the driveway.

They'll save me, she thought. *They'll let me in.*

She could hear the man's boots clatter onto the pavement behind her. She could hear his hard breathing, feel him as he closed the gap between them. Something inside her propelled her forward, past her burning muscles and pinching lungs, and she jumped over a shrub, her feet pounding across the pristine green lawn. The front door was only inches away.

Riley reached, feeling like her muscles were tearing, her

fingernails scraping the door. When she got traction, she pounded with her fists, mashed the doorbell. She could hear the stupid, slow chime gently ringing.

"Let me in!" she screamed. "Please let me in!"

She grabbed the knob and miraculously, the door fell open.

"Call the police! Call the police!" The tears were streaming down her face now, and everything that she ignored came surging back, all together, paralyzing her body in one aching mess. "Call the—"

Riley stopped. All the lights were blazing, and a few pristine pieces of living room furniture were set in the main window, but nobody was there. The kitchen was set up with a bowl of fake fruit on a shiny wooden table and a telephone on the counter.

She bolted for it.

Her fingers closed around the receiver and she dialed 9-1-1 without waiting for a dial tone.

Nothing happened.

"Hello? Hello?"

She yanked the phone and it plopped right off the counter, thunking to the hardwood floor below. It had no wires. No telephone jack.

Her hands started to shake.

A crash against the glass door in front of her snapped her attention, and Riley could see the man, his fists slamming against the door. Each slam shook the glass and rattled the teeth in Riley's head. The glare from the light cut across his face, and Riley knew that if she just stepped forward, she could see who he was—but she refused to step forward.

"Come on, Jane!"

She was close enough to see the spittle come out of his mouth. She took a staggering step back, feeling the phone digging into her ankle.

And then she was falling.

It happened in slow motion. She could see the roosters on the kitchen wallpaper arcing gently as her body went down, down. She felt the crush of her bones as she hit the floor, first her hip, then her shoulder, and finally her head. Somewhere, she heard the sickening smack of flesh against wood, and then the pain was pinballing through her. Her ears rang, and a blanket of red covered her eyes.

Vaguely, she heard footsteps. Then hands working their way under her arms. She felt the prick of her hair breaking as someone tried to gather her up. Riley knew she should fight. She knew she should scream. Those were the last thoughts she had before the darkness fell over her.

• • •

Riley opened her eyes and her body arced in pain. It screamed from her hip, from her arms; she felt like her lungs had been overinflated then popped.

"Mom?"

"Oh, Riley, thank God."

Riley blinked, trying to clear the fuzz from her head. "What happened? Where am I?"

"You're at home, in your bed. We were hoping you could tell us what happened."

She pinched her eyes shut, the evening coming back in

fragments. She remembered the man, the car, the clawing terror. "There was someone chasing me." Riley cleared her throat and her mother handed her a cup of water with a plastic straw.

"Take it easy."

"How did you find me?"

Her mother breathed in a deep sigh. "Someone from the realty office called your father's phone."

"And?"

She looked away. "Someone reported that there was a young woman running down the street, screaming. He said she went into one of the model homes."

Riley struggled to sit up. "Did they get him? The man who was chasing me, did they get him?"

Mrs. Spencer's eyes looked glassy and she blinked away tears. "There wasn't anyone chasing you, sweetie."

Riley's breath caught. "Yes, there was."

"The young man who called said he saw you run away from the house. He said you tried the door and then took off running. He didn't mention a man."

"Well then, he didn't see him. But he was in a black car and he knew my name." Riley clutched at the neck of her nightgown that seemed uncomfortably tight. "He knew her too. He was coming after me. He was pounding on the sliding glass door."

Riley's mother said nothing as a tear slid down her cheek.

"If you don't believe me, just go outside. There has to be tire marks and, and, he was pounding on the sliding glass door. He was screaming. He was spitting."

Her mother reached out and cupped her hand. "There was no one there, Riley."

She snatched her hand away. "Yes, there was."

"Why didn't you just come home?"

"Because I left my keys here. And Dad took my cell phone." Riley could hear the frustrated quiver in her voice. "You weren't here. The door was locked. I couldn't get in."

Riley watched her mother press her lips together and look away then slide Riley's backpack off her desk. She unzipped a pouch, and Riley's heart stopped. Her keys and her cell phone were nestled in the front pouch, just like they always were. She shook her head.

"No, they weren't there. They were here. I left my keys on the kitchen table and Dad took my phone."

"He gave it back to you last night."

"No, no, he didn't. I didn't have it."

"Riley, honey, did you stop taking your pills?"

Riley could feel the flush of heat over her cheeks. "My pills?"

Her mother dug into the backpack and produced the wadded-up Ziploc Riley used to hide the pills she spit out each morning.

Riley swallowed. "I don't like them."

"That's fine, honey, but you shouldn't have stopped cold turkey. It's dangerous. There are all sorts of side effects."

Fire burned in Riley's gut. "Like thinking I'm being chased? I was. I was!" She kicked off the covers and tried to stand up, but her legs were heavy and noodly. Her mother rushed toward her and helped her gently back to bed.

"Don't stand up. I've given you something to relax."

"What?" Riley's vision already started to blur. "You gave me drugs?"

Her mother stood up and pulled the blankets to Riley's chin, tucking them in all around her. "We've all had a rough day, Riley. Go to sleep." She straightened and smiled, her palm cool against Riley's forehead. "Don't you worry about anything. Your dad and I have it all taken care of."

• • •

The clattering of dishes in the sink woke Riley the next morning. Her muscles were raw and sore and her head throbbed in time with her heartbeat.

"Mom?" Riley took a tentative step then picked her way down the stairs. Her mother was scrubbing a dish, but she turned when Riley walked in.

"How are you feeling?"

"OK. Where's Dad?"

Riley's mom waggled a coffee mug. "Gone to get coffee. He really needed to clear his head. Riley, I—"

Riley stepped back, holding up a hand. "Can we not talk about it right now? My head is killing me."

Her mother sighed, exasperated. But there was something else too—exhaustion.

"Can I go for a walk?"

"That's not—"

"Please, Mom? Just around the block?"

"Ten minutes."

Riley nodded and scrambled for the door, ignoring the pain in her limbs. Someone had chased her; she wasn't going crazy. And she was going to prove it.

Riley crossed the street, crouching down on the blacktop and scrutinizing it. She followed the path the black car had taken until she reached the house where she had hidden. There was a litter of dirt across the driveway and Riley ran toward it, sure that it would have tracked the car's tire marks.

The dirt was undisturbed.

She searched around the house and found a trail of footprints—size seven and a half, hers. There was only one set. Riley dropped down on her hands and knees and began searching, inch by inch. She was vaguely aware of time passing or cars driving by, but she was desperate to find something—desperate to prove she wasn't crazy.

"Riley!"

Riley's head snapped up as her father coasted to a stop and got out of the car.

"Dad!"

His hand closed over her wrist. "Come on. We're going home."

Riley tried to pull back. "I don't want to."

Her father cut his eyes to her. There was something in them Riley had never seen before—something hard, something fierce. Fear zinged down her spine. "Dad?"

"Do you know how panicked we were yesterday? Your mother was sick. We asked you to trust us." He leveled his gaze at her. "I really hope you do."

Riley blinked into her father's eyes—mesmerized and paralyzed. She felt her feet moving. She fell into step behind him, his palm still closed over her wrist. He said nothing to her but he was standing too tall, too straight, and his posture spoke volumes. He was angry, frustrated, sad. His jaw was clenched, and Riley veered back, knowing better than to talk.

Instead, she let herself be led, closing her mind off to the wild possibilities that were ricocheting inside her skull: she was being led like a lamb to the slaughter. Like an unruly teen by her frustrated father. Like a victim with the man who stole her.

• • •

Riley sat in the front seat, staring silently out the windshield.

"Where did you go?" her father asked.

Riley pretended she didn't hear him.

"Did you talk to anyone?"

Again, silence.

"You're going to have to talk to me eventually, Ry."

She turned slowly, staring at her dad's profile. "So are you."

"We're going to explain everything in a second. But, Riley, honestly, you can't just go running off like that. Not you. Not now."

Riley was sure she felt her heartbeat slow. "Who's Tim?"

Her father's eyebrows went up. "Tim? I don't know any Tim. What are you taking about?"

Riley bit into her bottom lip, relishing the metallic taste of blood that filled her mouth. It was real. She wasn't sure anything else was.

"Why, Dad?"

"What?"

"Why the secrecy? Why the lies? If I'm really Jane—"

Her father's glare was sharp. "I want you to forget you ever heard that name, you hear me? Jane O'Leary is gone now."

Riley turned in her seat, her glare as fierce as her father's. "I'm right here."

Her father clapped a palm to his forehead and dragged it over the back of his head. Riley noticed that his hair was thinning, something she hadn't noticed before.

"Ry, you don't understand what you're dealing with. This isn't a silly teenage thing. You've got to believe me. You've got to trust us." He blew out a sigh that Riley swore hitched on a sob. "Please, honey, you've got to trust us."

Something stabbed at Riley's heart. This was her *father*. His hair was thinning and there were wrinkles around his eyes—not just when he smiled now, but all the time. She wanted to soften. She wanted all of this to go away so she could crawl in between her parents while they watched a black-and-white movie, eating popcorn while her father did some stupid impression.

But none of that was real.

Riley refused to cry. She spent the rest of the ride staring straight ahead, back ramrod straight, her teeth digging into her lips, begging not to cry.

• • •

They were only driving a few blocks, but it seemed to take forever. The asphalt seemed to peel on, inch after inch, going achingly slow. When they finally crested the slope in front of her, Riley suddenly wished the ride were longer.

Her heart started to speed up again, and her stomach folded in on itself. She played with the automatic window button, sliding the window all the way down, gulping in a few breaths of fresh, ocean-tinged air, and sliding the window closed again. They turned the corner onto Riley's street and ice water shot through her veins.

There was no one else in the neighborhood. Even the other house where a family lived was shut up tight. The sound of car doors slamming—Riley's and her father's—echoed against emptiness.

Riley's throat was dry and she found herself reaching out instinctively, grabbing for her dad. Her fingers found the edge of his sweater and she held it like she did as a small child, her fingertips brushing over his wrist.

"I'm scared, Dad."

She expected the word "dad" to sound wrong in her mouth—to look wrong on this man. But she felt more attached to him than ever.

He reached back and pulled Riley to him, crushing her in a tight hug.

"What's going on?" Riley whispered again.

"I'm so sorry, Ry," he breathed, kissing the top of her head.

TEN

Riley trailed behind her father, walking toward the house like a condemned traitor to a hanging. Halfway there, her father turned around and held his hand out to her. Riley rushed toward him and he pulled her into a hug. She wanted to rewind a week, back to when she was Riley Spencer and no one else, when she would skulk around her bedroom on Saturday nights because her over-protective parents wouldn't let her go anywhere. But time had passed, and her father had aged, and Riley Spencer had no idea who she was.

Her mother was waiting at the front door, her hands crossed in front of her chest, holding her elbows. Riley wondered if her mother had always been that fragile-looking, always been that fine-boned. Her eyes were red-rimmed but she smiled at Riley anyway—a smile that was half welcoming, half apologetic.

Riley's heart slammed. Stepping over the threshold into the house—her own house—seemed like an admission of something, a willingness to acknowledge that from that moment on, her life would never be the same.

Both her parents flanked her, ushering her into the room. She settled in the easy chair, her parents settling on either side of her. The birth certificate—Jane Elizabeth O'Leary's birth certificate—lay on the coffee table in the center of the room, in the center of everyone, but nobody acknowledged it.

"Riley, this birth certificate you found is yours. Your mother and I are your parents. Your real name is Jane Elizabeth O'Leary. Our real names are Seamus and Abigail."

There was a brief pause; Riley assumed it was to let her absorb what she already knew.

"So why am I Riley? Why are you Glen and Nadine?" Her eyes skidded over the birth certificate. "Why are you just telling me this now?"

"Fourteen years ago—back when you were still Jane, we lived just outside of Granite Cay."

Riley shrugged, her hands clasped in her lap. "OK, so?"

"There's a large Irish community there. You're Irish." Her mother's cheeks pinkened. "We're all Irish—the three of us. Your father was a woodworker. He made beautiful furniture. It's what his father did and his father before him back in Cork."

"Ry, I worked for a man who ran a large import-export business. He did remarkably well and was well-known in the American-Irish community as well as in communities back home. Families sent their children—kids about your age, maybe a little older—out to Alistair Foley. He gave them jobs, let them earn some money and learn a trade." Riley's father's eyes darkened. "At least that was what he said he was doing."

"Your father found out that Alistair was bringing kids in, but he wasn't letting them go back."

He nodded. "Right. At first we thought he was just making the kids he brought over work in the furniture store for free. That's what he said; that they worked for free, at first, to pay off his 'investment' in them. He paid their airfare over, the kids' living expenses while they were here, clothing, food. It seemed reasonable. The kids didn't complain."

Riley's mother cleared her throat then shifted her weight on the couch. "But these kids were never able to pay off their debt. In a sense, Alistair owned them. He brought them into this country as his nieces and nephews and then he exploited them."

Riley cut her eyes to her mother then back to her dad. "So that's why we moved away? That's why you changed my name? So your boss wouldn't make me work for free? That's—" She wanted to say it was dumb. It was ridiculous to be afraid of your boss. But one look at the consternation and fear on her parents' faces let Riley know that there was more—so much more.

"Alistair was trafficking in kids and young adults. He made money off them and threatened them if they ever told or tried to escape. He forced them to do illegal things and—he hurt them, Ry. Sometimes—sometimes the kids would just disappear. He'd say a kid that disappeared got a great new job somewhere or that he went back home."

Riley's mother crossed herself. "But they never made it home. Your father uncovered this, honey."

"I didn't have proof initially. At least not enough that could convict Alistair. But I brought it to the police anyway. I thought

I did it without Alistair's knowledge, but things got out of hand." Glen pressed his palms against his thighs, and Riley could see that there was a slight tremble in his fingers. It made her nervous. "Alistair had his hands in a lot of pots."

"The police promised they would take him down."

Riley gulped. "Did you have to do some kind of sting operation, Dad?"

Glen chuckled. "Nothing so exciting. I knew Alistair was laundering his trafficking money through the furniture store. I was able to get proof that he was embezzling, cooking the books, but still not enough for the trafficking conviction." He shrugged. "Most of the kids were too scared to talk."

"So he's just free? We're hiding and he's free?"

Riley's mother shook her head. "They were able to make some of the embezzling charges stick. But that only gave him a short time in prison."

"Long enough for us to get most of the kids somewhere safe."

"Most of them?"

"Alistair had a lot of people working under him, turnip. Even some in the police department."

Riley felt the dread well up inside her. She shook her head.

"No, no, I don't believe this. This is crazy. Are you trying to teach me a lesson or something? So I'll call you every time I—"

"I know it sounds crazy, Ry. And believe me, your mom and I hardly believed it ourselves."

"Once they had enough evidence, they took Alistair into custody. Your father was a key witness."

Riley brightened. "Yay, Dad. So you took down the bad guy."

Her parents exchanged an uncomfortable look. "Sort of. But not everyone was happy. We got death threats." Her mother drew a hand through Riley's hair.

"But it's over, right?"

"Alistair came to see me after he was released. He told me that since I had taken his children, he was going to take mine."

Her mother was holding back tears. "We wouldn't even take a chance of that happening, Ry."

"But couldn't you just pay him off or get him back in jail?"

"Even if we had the kind of money Alistair was used to making, it wouldn't have been any help. He didn't want money. He wanted revenge. He wanted you."

Her mother looked away. "He came for you one night."

"Alistair?"

"Alistair's men. Or the men above Alistair, we never knew. I was working then. I used to be a librarian. I went to work that night and you stayed home with your father."

"You liked my impressions then." Riley's dad's smile was wistful. Then he swallowed slowly, his neck corded and strained. "They came that night. Pounded down the door. They were like animals. There wasn't time to get out. I locked you in the closet." He hung his head. "I'm so sorry, Ry."

Riley felt her eyes widen. "The nightmares. The claustrophobia." Her lower lip started to tremble. "I remember. It was you." Her vision darkened and she was back in her nightmare, back in that closet, straining to see through those slats. She heard the thud. It

was her father's body on the ground. The acrid smell of blood…
Riley doubled over, heaving.

"I'm so sorry, Daddy."

"They left your father for dead. We contacted the police and
left that night. We left everything behind. We stayed in a hotel
until the authorities could get us situated with new identities,
new jobs—new lives. You were Riley Allen. We were the Spencers.
The O'Learys didn't exist anymore." Riley's mother splayed her
hand on her chest, her eyes brimming with tears. "We didn't
exist anymore."

"So, you had to rename me?"

Riley's mother shook her head. "We didn't have a choice."

"The Witness Protection Program gave our family new names,
new identities, new birth certificates, social security numbers—
everything. But the identities you assume with the program are
real people. Or they were."

Her mother put in, "Riley Allen Spencer was a baby boy. He was
born on your birthday—at least the one we've been celebrating for
the last thirteen years."

Riley stood up and then sat down again, feeling the intense need
to hyperventilate—or possibly pass out. She could see the worry in
her mother's eyes.

"Are you OK, hon?"

Riley nodded. The action was rote; she wasn't sure if she'd ever
be OK again.

"I need to get to school." She stood, her parents jumping up on
either side of her.

"Actually, Ry, you don't need to go to school today," her father told her. "You're already so late."

"Your father is right. It's probably better that you don't." Her eyes went over Riley's head and locked on Riley's father's. Riley was beginning to hate those looks—her parents exchanging them when they thought she wasn't looking, over her head. They may have told her the truth, but all these silent conversations let Riley know that what she was told was just the tip of the iceberg.

"Why don't you change into your sweats? I can make you a grilled cheese," her mother said. "You love grilled cheese when you're sick."

"I'm not sick. I'm going to school." Riley shook her head. "I want to. I want to—to process this."

I know who I am at school.

Riley's mother wrung her hands in front of her.

"Maybe Riley being around her friends—having a normal day—would be better for her. It's not like there has been a breach of security."

More silent conversation. Riley watched her father suck in a deep breath before he turned to her, his eyes clouded and locking on hers.

"You cannot mention this to anyone, Riley. It is incredibly important that you go to school today and act as if nothing—none of this, none of us"—he spread out his arm, indicating the whole room—"ever happened."

Riley's throat itched. She stood, grabbed her backpack, and hiked it up on her shoulder. "Like this never happened," she repeated. "Sure."

• • •

Classes had already started when Riley's father let her out in front of Hawthorne High. She turned, watching him drive away, watching his taillights fade into the distance before turning back to the sprawling school buildings. Without students milling about out front, their cars thudding with sound as they pulled into the lot, the school seemed ominous—although really, nothing about it had changed.

Nobody questioned Riley when she picked up her late pass. She walked down the silent hall, each step making her heart beat a little more smoothly, making her breath come a little more normally. *My school,* Riley thought. *I belong here. I'm Riley Allen Spencer and I'm a Hawthorne Hornet and I'm a junior. I'm not Jane Elizabeth O'Leary. I don't know who Jane Elizabeth O'Leary even is. She doesn't even exist.*

"Miss Spencer, so nice of you to join us." Mrs. Halloran greeted every late student the same way, and it was comforting to Riley. She went through the expected rush of heat on her cheeks and took her seat, letting Shelby hiss to her what she had missed.

"A total snoregasm," Shelby said. "And where were you yesterday? I called you a thousand times!"

Riley opened her mouth but Halloran cut in with a sharp look. Shelby looked away for a half second before hissing, "And by the way? You're just in time for a freaking pop quiz."

"Thank you for catching Miss Spencer up, Miss Webber," Mrs. Halloran said as she came down the aisle, sliding Riley's test paper onto her desk. Riley swallowed, feeling the butterfly wings start to flutter in her belly.

This is good, she thought. *This is normal. I always get butterflies before a test.*

Nothing happened at home. Nothing happened. Everything is regular.

Riley poised her pencil over the paper, her eyes skimming over the subject matter. *Red Badge of Courage. OK, OK, I totally know this.*

For the first time this morning, a smile broke across her lips. She zipped down the page, penciling in answers, glad they weren't buried in her brain under every question she had about her parents, about Jane. Then she went back to the top of the page and stopped. Top line. Top question: NAME.

The word throbbed on the page. Riley looked around. Every other student was writing, heads bent, pencils scratching.

Because they knew who they were.

The thought sickened—and terrified—her.

"Is there something wrong, Riley?"

Mrs. Halloran's eyes were on her, but Riley couldn't force her mouth to move. She shook her head and wrote the words—the name Riley Spencer.

If she wasn't anybody, she thought, she could be anyone.

But the name swam in front of her eyes. Her blood was pulsing again, this time through her ears and behind her eyes. She raised her hand.

"Mrs. Halloran? Can I be excused? I don't feel so well."

Shelby swung her head and grimaced. "You don't look so good."

Riley leaned over. "I feel horrible."

"Are you ever going to tell me what happened?"

Mrs. Halloran strode down the aisle and handed Riley a pink hall pass. "Riley, you can go to the nurse. Shelby, you can get back to work."

Riley felt dizzy and queasy the second she stood up. She edged her way out of the classroom, trying to remind herself how to walk. She picked up speed as she went down the hallway. When she got to the door of the nurse's office, she stopped then abruptly turned around.

She pushed through the double doors outside the commons, letting the cool mist of the morning air break over her. She doubled over, huffing huge gulps, hoping that the excess oxygen would clear the gray blur from her head or, at the very least, wake her up.

No such luck.

Riley straightened, her eyes zeroing in on the visitors parking lot where a car was parked dead center. It was a dark blue sedan— nothing special, nothing sinister—and a man was sitting behind the wheel.

Riley's heart started to thud. The air that she sucked in was zapped from her lungs. She squinted. Was the driver looking at her too?

No.

She was paranoid. The guy was probably someone's dad, waiting for his kid to come out after being suspended or barfing in the biology lab.

He wasn't a police officer, a detective, a criminal. He wasn't one of "them."

No one knew who she was.

Her pulse throbbed. *Except for the man from last night.* She shuddered. *The man who didn't exist.*

She pressed herself against the doors, relishing the cold of the glass as it seeped through her T-shirt. It grounded her.

"I'm going crazy," Riley muttered to herself.

She zipped her hoodie up to her neck and cut across the commons. When she heard the rev of a car engine, she forced herself not to look back, not to check if the blue sedan pulled out. She didn't have a plan other than to move. Walk. Push one foot in front of the other. That was what she was concentrating on when the blue sedan pulled up right beside her.

ELEVEN

The sedan slowed to match Riley's pace, and Riley's mind went into hyperdrive. *Stop. Run. Turn around.*

"Riley Spencer?" The driver of the sedan leaned against his door toward her, his face shadowed by the sunlight breaking through the windshield.

Riley's heart lodged in her throat. It wasn't the man from the previous night.

It was Tim.

"I just want to talk to you."

Riley slowed but sidestepped further away from the car.

"I know who you really are, Jane, and your parents are lying to you. They're trying to brainwash you. I know because they did it to me."

Riley's parents' words rolled through her head, searing like hot lava.

"They were forcing kids to work. They got caught. My stepdad, Alistair—"

Electricity bolted through Riley, and her head snapped toward Tim.

"Do you remember Alistair Foley, Jane? He blew the whistle. Come on, we need to—"

Tim reached out the window, his clawed fingertips brushing Riley's arm as she snapped it away.

Immediately, her body took over. Her saliva soured and adrenaline shot through her system. Suddenly, her thighs were burning. Heart thundering. Eyes watering.

She was running.

It could have been her own scream or the screech of the blue sedan's tires. Whatever it was, it tore through her skull and blanketed out every other thing around her. All Riley knew was that the sidewalk was ending and the car next to her was chewing up the street. The car turned in front of her but the adrenaline coursing through her veins was still vaulting her forward. She jumped, the pads of her fingers digging into the hood of the car. The door kicked open and the driver was out as Riley scrambled over the hood. He lunged for her, his fingers lacing through her hair as it trailed behind her. She felt the sting of the pull, heard the strands as they tore out, burning her scalp.

She winced. Her feet hit the ground and another car screeched to a stop in front of her.

"Get in."

Riley's heart stopped when her feet did.

"Get in!" JD repeated, yanking her arm.

Somehow, she opened the door. Somehow, she sat down.

"Wha—how did you know?" Riley managed as JD slammed on the gas.

"Lucky guess," he said, jaw set hard.

Riley slammed back in her seat and fumbled for her seat belt, her eyes checking the rearview mirror, catching the sedan behind them. The driver was staring straight forward. There was a deep frown cut into his face, and though his eyes were hidden behind dark glasses, Riley was sure they were boring through JD's back windshield, trying to cut through her.

"He's following us! What are we going to do?"

JD didn't answer; he just drove. He cut across streets and turned down ones Riley didn't even know existed. Within moments, the blue sedan dropped out of view.

Once they were going at a normal pace—obeying traffic laws and stop signs—JD turned to her. "Are you going to tell me what that was about?" His words were clipped, voice tinged with exasperation.

Riley was still struggling to breathe. She clamped a hand over her mouth, fairly certain her heart would pop out if she tried to speak. She looked at JD and tried to force her shoulders to shrug, but she was completely disconnected. She expected JD to grumble at her or kick her out of his car. Instead, he reached into the backseat and handed her a semi-warm water bottle.

She cracked the seal and drank gratefully.

Finally, "Thank you. For…everything."

JD grinned despite his previous veneer. "Hey, thank you. I'm always looking for a little adventure in my life."

Riley folded herself forward, tucking her head between her legs and rolling the water bottle over the back of her neck. "If I ever ask for adventure in my life ever again, promise you'll shoot me."

"Will do."

She popped her head back up as the car slowed down and scanned the horizon. "Where are we?"

Branches thunked against the rooftop and gravel popped under the tires until JD pushed the car into park. "Nowhere. Just an old frontage road. Seriously, Ry, what is going on with you?"

She swallowed hard. "Someone tried to attack me last night."

"It seems like someone tried to attack you just now."

Riley gritted her teeth. "I think someone is following me. I think someone is—is trying to hurt me. For revenge." It sounded as crazy in her mind as it did out of her mouth.

"And this has to do with Jane?"

Riley perked up. "Jane. You said you found Jane's brother, Tim."

Jane and Tim O'Leary were two separate entities to Riley. She wasn't Jane O'Leary and this whole thing wasn't happening.

"Maybe. I mean, at least someone claiming to be her brother."

Riley's breath caught in her throat. She didn't want to be Jane. She didn't want to be Jane with a brother. Tim flashed in her eyes—his blue eyes that nearly matched hers, his strawberry blond hair just a few shades darker.

I can't believe a stranger over my own parents. They only lied to me to keep me safe—because they had to.

"Why do you say someone claiming to be her brother? I mean, why would someone claim that?"

JD shrugged. "I don't know. Maybe he wants Jane's money or there's an inheritance or something."

Riley thought of her nice home, her parents' nice cars. They were comfortable, but they weren't rich. At least not rich enough to lie over.

"Who knows? People pretend to be other people for all sorts of crazy-ass reasons."

Her first instinct was negative, but now she wasn't really sure.

"So what did you find out about this Tim guy?"

JD twisted in his seat and dug in his backpack. "This."

He hand Riley a curl-edged piece of printer paper, and Riley wished he hadn't. She didn't recognize the web address, but she recognized the picture—it was the man from the mall.

Riley read the message. "Looking for my sister JANE E. O'LEARY. Missing since June 1996 from/around Granite Cay, Oregon." There was a number to call and a smattering of vaguely recognizable clues: *Has blue eyes. Probably red to light red hair.*

Riley's throat went immediately dry. She thought of her parents, of Tim, cruising by her in the blue sedan.

"I don't think this is right," she said, letting the paper flutter to the floor. "Where did you find it again?"

"Just ran some searches. It's weird; it was the only thing I found on her."

Riley nodded, certain she had upturned every Internet stone. "Tim" wasn't her brother.

Maybe Tim was Alastair?

The thought made her blood run cold.

Shelby's ringtone blared through the silent cab.

"Hey," Shelby yelled into the phone, "where are you?"

Riley swallowed hard then took a swig from her water bottle. "Uh, I wasn't feeling well."

"Duh, dork, I was sitting in class with you. I've been looking everywhere for you. You left all your stuff."

"I totally forgot."

"I picked up your jacket and backpack. Are you at home? You want me to swing it by?"

"No!" She sat up straighter. "I mean, no, it's OK, you don't have to do that. I'm not home—"

"I can bring it by later. School just got out. Where are you? And if you're off on some mysterious sexcapade, I'm stealing your jacket and throwing your backpack in the dumpster. Well, I'm stealing your jacket, your trig homework, your lip gloss, and your emergency twenty, but then I'm ditching the rest."

"How did you know about my emergency twenty bucks?"

"Everyone is supposed to have an emergency twenty, Ry. You're the only person I know who actually does. Where are you again?"

Riley chewed the inside of her lip and scanned her surroundings, as if something appropriate to tell Shelby would sprout out of the sunbaked earth.

"The doctor."

Riley had never lied to Shelby before, and now the word tasted sour in her mouth.

"Oh." Shelby's voice immediately took on the parental edge she used when babysitting her siblings. "Is it serious?"

Guilt welled in Riley's gut. "No—no. I think I might have just gotten some kind of flu or food poisoning or something. Would you mind just hanging on to my backpack and coat for the night?" She went back to tracing the stitch line on her jeans. "The way I'm feeling, it's not like I'll be doing any homework anyway."

That wasn't a lie.

"Yeah, no problem. But seriously, I'm wearing this jacket. And I might borrow your backpack too. Yours doesn't have any food stains on it."

"Fine, but if it smells like Ruffles when I get it back…"

Riley clicked the phone shut, feeling half relaxed and comfortable, half a horrible friend for lying to Shelby and making her schlep her stuff home.

JD sat up. "We should probably be getting back."

Riley felt herself frown. "Already?"

"School's out. Don't your parents have some sort of tracking device on you once the bell rings?"

"Very funny." Riley knew that if she didn't come home immediately, her parents would be calling, wondering, panicked—and that made her want to stay out.

"Didn't you say something about a pizza?"

JD had just steered the car onto the road when the calls started. Riley looked at the readout: MOM. The word throbbed there, dancing to the electronic ringtone. *Mrs. O'Leary…*

JD jutted his chin toward the phone in Riley's hand. "Aren't you going to get that?"

Riley closed her eyes and her mother flashed in her mind. In a second, her image was gone and a minute angry flame flared up. *If they had just told me the truth…*

"No." She smiled at JD across the seat, feeling mysterious and dangerous and comfortable. The blue sedan pricked at the edges of her mind, but Riley didn't want to think about it. She only wanted to think about being there in the cab of JD's car, where she was a normal kid playing hooky.

JD flipped on his blinker, heading toward the school.

"Is your car in the lot?"

Riley froze. "No, actually, I got a ride this morning."

"No big, I'll drop you off at home."

Dread welled up inside her. "At home? No, you don't have to do that." She was already in more trouble than she could fathom; coming home with JD might push her parents completely over the edge.

"So, what? Bus station? Want to grab another train and see where it takes us?" He wasn't smiling, but his tone was playful. "Although I don't know any buses or trains that go all the way out to the Blackwood Hills Estates."

Riley pinched her top lip. "How do you know where I live?"

JD shifted his weight, and the car seemed to slide into a higher gear. He zeroed in on the road in front of him while Riley zeroed in on his right ear. "You told me earlier," he said nonchalantly.

Riley tried to replay all the conversations she'd had with JD over the past week, but they jumbled and swirled with the stern look of her father and the nervous words of her mother. *Did I tell him where I lived?*

She glanced at JD's profile once more, a tiny niggle of fear creeping up the back of her neck.

No, she commanded. *Stop being paranoid.*

"How about you just drop me off up at the gate? It takes forever once you get into the development."

JD smoothly made the turn onto the road that led to the estates. "It's no problem. No one's expecting me home or anything."

Riley felt herself shift over on her seat, putting an extra quarter inch of distance between herself and JD. He chose that moment to glance over at her, at the shift of her body. The hurt was evident in his eyes.

"It's not like I'm trying to kidnap you."

"I didn't mean—I mean, what are you talking about? I didn't do anything."

She could almost see the cogs working in JD's head. He leaned in as if to say something, thought better of it, and stepped on the gas. When they arrived at the wrought-iron gates of the Blackwood Hills Estates, Riley put her hand on the door handle the second JD slowed.

"This is fine. Thanks." She opened the door before he could protest, before he could turn down the street that led to Riley's house.

Riley jogged toward her house, not bothering to look over her shoulder to see whether or not JD was still parked at the gate. Her sneakers smacked against the concrete, the soft thuds echoing through the empty street as a slow, steady drizzle started overhead. As she rounded the corner to her house, Riley pinched her eyes closed, hoping against hope that when she opened them, everything would be back to normal: her front yard would still be a rocky, muddy mess with the orange spray-painted outline of where her mom intended to plant birch trees and lay sod, the driveway and sidewalks would be pristine and empty—no stray cars, no flashing lights, no cops waiting just inside the door. When she opened her eyes, she was standing in the middle of the street, raindrops breaking on her head and dribbling in rivulets into her eyes. But even through the blur of rainwater, Riley could see that nothing was the same—her once welcoming house now looked foreign and strange, the windows her mother had decorated with frilly lace curtains were gray and ominous as blurred shadows walked jerkily in front of them. Two strange cars were parked out front.

Her cell phone chirped.

"I'm right outside, Dad," Riley muttered into it.

She strode up the walk and sucked in a sharp breath, the icy air lancing her lungs and making them ache.

"Hey," Riley said softly.

Her mother rushed across the room and gathered Riley into her arms, hugging her tightly. The act should have been comforting—mother loving daughter—but it struck a cold fear in Riley. She shook her mother off and then immediately regretted it, noticing the heavy bags and redness underneath her eyes.

"Where have you been?"

"School," Riley said with a shrug.

Her mother's eyebrows went up. "This late?"

"I had to make up for being late this morning."

The tension in the room seemed to drop down a notch.

"How was school?" her father wanted to know.

Riley wanted to laugh. Her mother just gave her her normal after-school hug. Her father asked how her day was, like he did pretty much every other day of Riley's life.

But it wasn't Riley's life anymore. All three of them were actors playing a role. All three pretending, trying to fool the other, trying to deceive each other into this façade of regular, suburban, tract-home life.

Riley's ears pricked when she heard male and female voices in low, murmured conversation in the next room.

"Who's that? Who's here?"

Her father paled. Her mother pressed her lips together in what Riley was beginning to recognize as her "we're really sorry to tell you this" smile.

"That's Gavin Hempstead and Gail Thorpe." Her mother let the statement stand as though Riley had heard the names before, as though that was all the explanation she'd need.

"OK, but *who* are they and why are they here?"

Mrs. Spencer turned away and Riley was sure she saw tears rimming in her mother's bottom lashes.

"Gail is an FBI agent and Gavin is a U.S. Marshal. They're helping us out."

Riley's eyebrows disappeared into her bangs. "Helping us out? Why do we need help? We're in the Witness Protection Program, we live here, I'm not Jane O'Leary. End of story, right? It's not like I told anyone." She could hear the tinny desperation in her own voice, but Riley kept talking, trying to convince her parents, or herself, that everything was fine.

"Detective Thorpe is worried that there may have been some breaches in our security."

Riley plopped down on the couch, her head spinning. *Breaches in security? Had that really come out of my dad's mouth?*

"What does that mean? What's that supposed to mean?"

"Riley—" Her mother had her hand on her shoulder when the door that separated the kitchen from the living room swung open. Gail Thorpe came out first, looking nothing like the toned FBI agents Riley knew from television. She was slightly stout with hair somewhere between stone-gray and brown that was pulled back into a no-nonsense bun pinned at the nape of her neck. She was wearing a skirt suit, but the jacket was slightly ill-fitting and the skirt—not pencil thin or thigh high—was boxy and knee length. Instead of stilettos, Agent Thorpe wore brown loafers with thick rubber soles. Riley was so busy scrutinizing Agent Thorpe—who came toward Riley with an extended hand and a friendly smile, that she almost didn't notice the man coming out of the kitchen behind her.

"Nice to meet you Riley, I'm Agent Thorpe, but please call me Gail. And this"—she turned to gesture and Riley stood stone still, feeling her veins fill with cement—"is U.S. Marshal Hempstead."

Mr. Hempstead nodded at Gail then brushed in front of her, offering Riley a hand.

But Riley didn't move.

He looked different, somehow, standing in her living room. The man from the train station. He broke into a soft grin while Riley stared, but all she could see was his hard eyes drilling into her at the hospital. The insistent way he asked for her name in the street. How he said he was a doctor.

"Riley," her mother said in a half whisper, "stop staring, you're being rude."

"That's OK," Gavin said, his hand dropping to his side. "I'm sure this is a lot for Riley to take in." He didn't break eye contact or mention that they had previously met. Riley wondered if his gaze was a silent promise or a warning.

Riley shifted her weight from foot to foot and forced herself to mumble, "Hello."

"Why don't you sit down, Riley?" Gail asked.

Over the last twelve hours, Riley realized she hated those words. Nothing positive ever came out of an adult telling a kid to "sit down." She looked from her parents to Gail, and the gray static in her head started up again. She pressed her hands over her ears.

"I don't want to know."

Her father's large hand circled over Riley's wrist, making hers look like a child's. "You have to, turnip. It's important."

Riley knew her eyes were glassy. She blinked furiously. "Why are they here?"

Her mother's sharp intake of breath cut through the static in her head. "Actually, hon, Agent Thorpe—Gail—and Mr. Hempstead want to help us."

Riley's knees buckled and she flopped onto the couch. "Want to help us how?"

Mr. Hempstead perched on the arm of the couch and stared

Riley down. His face was relaxed, not unkind, but still it shot ice water down her spine.

From the wing chair across the room, Gail cleared her throat.

"Do you know what a U.S. Marshal is?"

Riley blinked, already on edge, already annoyed at the patronizing sound of Gail's voice.

"Of course I know what a marshal is."

"I am a supervisory deputy U.S. Marshal. I've been helping you and your parents for the past fourteen years."

"Let me get you another cup of coffee, Gail." Riley's mother stood up, and Gail followed right behind her.

"Oh, Nadine, I can do that."

Riley swung her head from her mother to her father, and then up at Deputy Hempstead. She felt like a stranger in her own living room, like the sole audience member of an incredibly bizarre play.

"So you've always known him?" Riley asked her father. "And her?"

"I've only just met Deputy Hempstead and your parents." It was Gail now, addressing Riley as she walked in through the swinging kitchen door. Riley hated Gail's familiarity with her house, with her family. When Gail and the deputy shared respectful acknowledgment, Riley kind of wanted to vomit. But she swallowed hard instead, focusing on a scuff mark on the wall across from her.

"Gavin has handled our case since the beginning. Dad checks in with him every month."

"Wait—he's handled our *case*?" Riley knew her lips moved, but she wasn't sure that any sound actually came out.

"Our family," her father corrected.

Could we even be called that?

"I was in charge of getting you settled, getting your new identi-ties, and keeping all of you"—his dark eyes scanned across the three of them—"safe."

Riley blinked and blinked. Gavin's smile was familiar—and it was genial and friendly—but she couldn't help but see something sinister in the grin, something evil in his eyes.

He was a liar.

They were all liars.

And now they were forcing her to be one.

TWELVE

Riley zoned in and out while the adults talked over her head. At some point, her mother started cooking and Riley set the dining room table with extra plates for Gail and the deputy. Her mother served spaghetti, and everyone sat around making ridiculous small talk about weather and sports scores.

Riley's cell phone started to blare out Shelby's ringtone, a spastic circus beat cutting through the white noise in the room. Deputy Hempstead, Riley's parents, and Gail all stared at the thing as though it were a bomb. Riley snatched it up and thumbed it to silent.

"Sorry," she breathed.

The adults went back to staring at each other around the dining table, and Riley went back to poking at the spaghetti on her plate. It was cold, and the cheese had congealed with everything else, so each time she stabbed a fork into it, the whole thing moved together.

"I'd like to get you out as soon as possible," Deputy Hempstead said. "There hasn't been a breach in security as far as we can tell, but I'm not in the business of sitting around and waiting for things to happen."

"How long?" her mother asked.

"End of the week at the latest."

Her father nodded and poked at his dinner. "Yeah, I think that's advisable."

"We've already alerted the FBI and they're actively searching for new identities for each of you."

Riley's head snapped up, her fork clattering to her plate. "What?"

"Our location and our identities have possibly been discovered, Ry. We're going to have to change them."

Riley felt her mouth drop open. "You mean move?"

Her mother forced a smile. "A new life. A new life! I won't have to deal with flu season after all."

Riley felt her mouth drop open. "Dad—Mom, you studied so hard to become a nurse. You can't just leave! You can't just leave in the middle of the school year. The kids are going to wonder what happened to you. Dad, you can't let this happen! Mom worked so hard." Her heart was beating hard, the few bites of pasta that she had eaten sitting like a cold, hard fist in her gut. "Tell them, Dad."

Her father's fake smile mirrored her mother. "Who knows? Maybe our new house will have a swimming pool."

"A swimming pool is supposed to make up for you dragging me out of my life? I don't want to move. I don't want to run away. I don't want to *be* someone else!"

"Riley—"

"How do we even know they care about us anymore? They've probably moved on or at least forgotten and don't care about us."

Her father pressed his lips together, the muscle in his jaw jumping. "That's not how it works, Riley. These kinds of people don't just forget things."

Riley could feel the sting of tears behind her eyes. She felt them break over her cheeks too, but by that time, she didn't care. She would have to leave. She would have to leave Shelby and JD and school.

"I'm not leaving," Riley said, standing. "You can't make me go. I'll stay here. I'll stay with Shelby's family."

"Even if that were possible, Ry, if you were to stay, we couldn't ever contact each other."

The realization hit Riley like a fist in the gut. "Ever?"

"We can't have any links. We can't have any ties from this life that could be traced. Which means, when we go—"

Riley's cell phone started to blare again and she instinctively went to at least pick it up, but her dad pinned her with a look. "Not now."

"But it's just Shelby."

The deputy stared her down. "Your dad is right. You should probably give me your phone."

Gail broke in. "Do you have accounts on social networking sites?"

Riley looked from her mother to her father, hoping that one of them would jump in.

"Everyone's online," she said slowly, licking her lips.

"We'll have someone delete your pages."

"What? Why?"

Hempstead's cell phone went next, a curt, conventional ring.

His conversation was just as curt and conventional. Riley strained to hear, but his side was mostly "uh-huhs" and "yeses."

"The FBI has secured new identities and a new residence for you." He smiled as though he were telling the family something positive. Riley gaped, expecting her parents to jump up, to protest, to say they appreciated it, but everything was going to be just fine.

No one did.

Riley launched herself off her chair. "So that's it, we're moving? I have to give up my cell phone and my Tumblr and everything *and* we're moving? Where? Why? Nothing happened. You said that there isn't any threat."

"I said there hasn't been any threat yet. That doesn't mean that there won't be."

Her father stood up. "Riley—" He reached out for her, but she dodged his arm, feeling hot tears pricking behind her eyes. She looked up at him, anger coloring her cheeks.

"Didn't you even think about us? Your family?" The tears started to fall, hot and heavy. "I don't want to move. I don't want to run away or be someone else again. I want to be normal and do normal things!" Her voice was getting high and sharp. No one ever yelled in their house, but Riley didn't care. "I'm not going to move. I didn't ask for any of this!"

Riley's mother stepped in, the set of her jaw stern. "None of us did, Riley. There wasn't any choice."

Riley's breath was coming in short bursts that pushed against her chest. "You could have chosen not to lie to me."

Her father took a steadying breath. "You didn't know any different. We thought it would be easier—and safer—for you."

"But my life—you ruined my life! I can't do anything. I can't go out for cheerleading—"

"And your father and I can't see or talk to our family. It's been hard on all of us, Ry. We had to leave our home and nearly everything in it in the middle of the night. We could only take what we could carry. I wasn't supposed to take the birth certificate." Her voice broke on the last words. "I shouldn't have. We were the Spencers from California. Your father ran a print shop. I was a stay-at-home mom and you were Riley Allen Spencer." Riley's mother gave Riley a half smile as tears rolled down her cheeks.

"And I wasn't named after your friend or your family. I was named after a dead baby." A sob broke in Riley's chest. "And now you're going to make me do it again."

"If there was any other way, turnip…"

Riley felt herself flinch. Even her father's pet name for her—usually so reassuring, annoying but reassuring—sounded wrong. Did the FBI tell him to call her that? Is that what the *real* Riley Allen was called? She shuddered, the tears coming harder.

"I'm sorry, Ry-Pie."

The adults moved around the room doing things Riley couldn't focus on. She sat there, silent, pressing her thin shoulders back against the cool wood of the high-backed dining room chair. Shelby called three more times; Riley only knew because she switched the phone to vibrate and shoved it under her leg as she sat, staring. Eventually, her mother came and patted her on the back, saying something in the soothing voice she used when Riley was sick. Riley let her heap some more spaghetti onto her plate. She eyed her father, and he offered a small smile then went back to eating. She wanted to look away from him but couldn't tear her eyes away. She stared at his bent head as he ate.

Riley's cell phone went again, this time thudding wildly as it flopped onto the ground.

"Sorry," she breathed. She glanced down at the readout, her eyebrows going up. It wasn't Shelby this time; it was JD. Riley looked around the table and knew she didn't dare answer.

Deputy Hempstead carefully set down his knife and fork, lacing his fingers together. "Your service is going off tomorrow. I'm sorry, Ry, but it's safer this way."

"And one day I'll understand," Riley muttered under her breath.

"What was that?"

"Right. Cell service off tomorrow. Can I at least tell my friends they can call the house or is that taboo too?"

The muscle in her father's jaw jumped and Riley knew the answer.

"So that service is going off too. What am I supposed to tell my friends?"

"You're not going to tell them anything, Ry." Her father's eyes were dark and fierce, and Riley felt her heartbeat speed up. "Understand?"

She didn't but nodded anyway.

"I won't be your handler at your new location," Deputy Hempstead said.

Riley stared at her spaghetti. "It doesn't matter. I'm not moving."

Gail cleared her throat and put her hand on Riley's. "Jane—"

Riley snapped. "Don't call me that! I'm not Jane—I've never been Jane! My name is Riley."

"Calm down, Riley." Her father was standing, his cheeks flushed. He, more than anyone Riley knew, hated confrontation. "It's going to be OK."

"I know this can't be easy, Riley"—Gail carefully enunciated her name—"but you really don't have a choice. You'll make new friends—"

Anger bubbled under Riley's skin. "This is not about my friends, *Gail*, this is about *my life*."

"Riley Allen Spencer! Gail is a guest in our home. You will not speak to her like that." Her father's eyes were sharp, his nostrils slightly flared.

A tense silence filled the room.

"Why don't you go up to your room and get a few things together?" Riley's mother may have been talking to her, but she didn't look up from her plate.

Riley stomped up the stairs and slammed her bedroom door. She flopped on the floor and yanked out her laptop, staring at the throbbing cursor on the search engine bar.

She started this.

She could finish it.

Before she could consider how she was going to finish the ordeal, her phone blasted again.

"My God," Riley grumbled. "Shel?"

"Uh, no, it's JD. I take it you haven't seen the news."

Riley pulled her hand over her face, thumbing away the last of her tears. "That's a weird hello."

"Turn on the TV, Ry. Channel eight."

"Fine." Riley cradled the phone against her shoulder and flicked on the television. The smiling, perfectly coifed anchor people grinned out at her. "What am I supposed to be looking at? I kind of don't care if it's supposed to rain tomorrow—"

The anchor woman's smooth expression immediately dropped into one of practiced sympathy, and the little Hawthorne High Hornet icon filled a box over her right shoulder.

"A Hawthorne High student was the victim of a hit-and-run today at the intersection of West and Falia. The car, described as a late model dark-colored sedan, was traveling east when it struck the female student." The anchorwoman looked down at her papers but Riley already knew the name she was going to say. "Junior Shelby Webber is in critical condition."

The picture switched to a uniformed officer standing behind a podium, a doctor to his left as they somberly restated the facts—an unidentified sedan, high rate of speed, victim in critical condition.

Riley sucked in a breath. "Oh my God."

The officer kept talking, blathering about a number to call if you had any additional information while the picture changed again. This time it was the intersection at West and Falia—just a few blocks from where JD had picked up Riley hours earlier. Riley's chest tightened as she saw students and teachers huddled behind a yellow-taped police line, but it was what was in the intersection, strewn like forgotten garbage, that made the bile rush up the back of her throat: the crushed bumper of the blue sedan, the red smear of blood on the concrete, and Riley's backpack, the color sullied from a drag across the street.

Riley didn't remember dropping the phone or slamming the television off. She didn't remember anything as she bent over the toilet, retching.

Tim had been driving a sedan.

Was it black? Blue?

He said he was her brother. He said he wanted to help her.

Riley stifled a sob.

Shelby had Riley's coat, had her backpack—and didn't look all that different from Riley. Riley flushed the toilet and rinsed out her mouth then sunk to her knees. The tears started again, and she crumpled to the floor, her burning cheek cooled by the chilled tile. A shudder ran through her body. Her teeth chattered. She pulled a bath towel from the bar and snuck under it, pulling her knees up to her chest.

It was because of her.

The sedan had wanted her and had hit Shelby instead.

Riley only lay on the floor a few minutes before the canned voice on her cell phone started her message: *if you'd like to make a call, please hang up and dial again.*

The second Riley—with shaking, weak fingers—mashed the END CALL button, the phone blared again.

"H—he—hello?"

"Are you OK?"

Riley swallowed then winced, her saliva like sandpaper running over her raw throat. "Did you find out about this on the news or did someone tell you? Do you know anything more?"

"No," JD said on a sigh. "My mom saw the police tape when she was driving home. And I don't know anything else about Shelby's condition. But I'm about to find out." A pause. "Ry, the blue sedan—that was the car that was following you, right?"

But Riley couldn't answer. Guilty tears choked the words in her throat.

"Be outside the gate in twenty minutes."

As JD clicked off the phone, Riley started to pace.

I need to tell them about Tim. He's obviously dangerous.

If Tim was the one who hit her.

Doubts crept into her head; there were a thousand sedans in Crescent City. They really don't know the color.

Why am I protecting him?

Riley went for the door and was on the top of the stairs when she heard the chatter downstairs.

"Does it really have to be this soon?" her mother was saying.

"It doesn't really have to be, but it's for the best. If you're worried about Riley, she'll adjust. Most teenagers get over it once they make some friends."

Anger roiled in Riley's belly. How dare Deputy Hempstead talk so dismissively about her? How dare he talk about her at all?

Riley pulled on a fresh sweatshirt and yanked her hair into a ponytail. Her eyes and nose were red and puffy, but there wasn't enough makeup in the world to change that, and frankly, Riley didn't care.

Maybe the accident wasn't so bad, Riley told herself as she tried to breathe deeply. *The news was always blowing things out of proportion.* Even as she thought it, Riley knew it wasn't true. She bit her lip and speed-dialed Shelby's number. She heard the crackle of canned air on Shelby's end.

No ring.

No dial tone.

Nothing but dead air.

THIRTEEN

The new house may have had crappy cell service and a just-north-of-nowhere area code, but it did have one major plus: the giant heap of dirt that cushioned Riley's landing when she crossed her fingers, closed her eyes, and jumped out of her second-story window.

Before the jail break, her parents were pacing and murmuring things, and Gail and the deputy were studying something intently—probably a list of all the basic teenage amenities that he was planning on taking away from Riley "for her own safety." Thinking of her parents' betrayal vaulted Riley forward once her feet hit the ground. She kept to the wrought-iron fencing lining the estates, her lungs burning, the cold slapping at the tears as they ran down her face.

JD was leaning against his car when Riley made it to the front gate. He was bathed in a yellow glow from the streetlight above, looking very much James Dean. The image called up memories of snuggling on the couch with her parents, and Riley stomped it away.

"She's at Crescent General and she's out of ICU," JD said, opening the door for Riley.

She dove inside, aching as the seconds it took for JD to get in the car and continue his story seemed to stretch on for eons.

"And? Do they know anything? Is she OK?"

JD started up the engine and floored the gas pedal. Riley could hear the tires spin, kicking up dirt and gravel before they caught hold of the road. Finally she could breathe.

"So?"

JD cleared his throat. "She's stable."

"Stable means not dead, right?"

"Hey." JD awkwardly patted the top of her hand then put his back on the wheel. "Relax. She's going to be OK. It's going to take a while but she's going to be fine."

Riley pressed herself back in her seat, her body sagging, aching muscles protesting against any motion at all. "I'm just so scared for her."

"It's going to be OK," JD said again.

Riley glanced over the console, examining JD's profile. The moonlight illuminated his strong forehead and nose, showing off the stern set of his jaw. Riley stiffened again.

"There's something you're not telling me."

JD shrugged, not taking his eyes off the road. "I'm telling you everything I know."

"Who gave you the information?"

"Ry, I'm not the one who's been lying to you."

Riley crossed her arms in front of her chest, icy fingers of suspicion walking down her spinal column. "Who told you, JD?"

He blew out a sigh that was part exasperation, part exhaustion. "I dated Shelby's sister for a while, OK?"

"Which one? Tru?"

JD guided the car over a smooth turn. "Yeah."

"She's, like, twenty!"

"Yeah, well, we dated when she was, like, seventeen."

Riley gaped. "You were fourteen then! That's disgusting."

"I was fifteen, almost sixteen."

"You're older than me?"

"Eighteen two weeks ago."

"Oh." Riley sat back again. "Happy birthday."

"Meaningful. Anyway, I called Tru and she told me about Shelby and the accident."

"What about the accident?"

JD went back to that hard expression, staring directly out the front windshield, his hands gripping the steering wheel as if he wasn't driving on a straight, freshly paved road.

"It wasn't just a regular sedan kind of car that hit her, was it? It was the blue one. The one that Tim was driving?"

"Tim?" JD looked surprised.

Riley shook her head and looked imploringly at JD.

He swallowed hard, pausing for a beat. "The witnesses say the sedan was circling the school. It started to follow Shelby."

Riley nodded, numbness creeping into her finger and toes.

"It sped up when she entered the crosswalk."

Riley's stomach folded in on itself and she thought she was going to be sick again. "Sped up?"

"He hit her once…" JD's voice trailed off and Riley's heartbeat sped up. "She fell; she hit the road." He cleared his throat. "And then he backed over her."

Riley felt the bile burning at the back of her throat. Her vision was suddenly blurry, and the windshield, the dashboard in front of her—everything—disappeared behind her tears.

"They said he was gearing up to do it again, but he must have realized he'd be penned in if he went that direction. He turned around and sped off."

Riley folded over, pressing her head between her knees. "Oh God."

"It was all really quick."

Riley popped back up. "But there were witnesses. And it takes time to put a car in reverse. Why didn't someone help her? Why didn't someone stop him?"

The night broke, and a smatter of rain hit the hood of the car. The drops on the windshield cast a mottled shadow over JD's face when Riley turned to look at him.

"I don't know, Riley."

Panic tightened her chest.

Her fault.

"Someone must have gotten a license plate, right? Or someone filmed it or took a picture?"

JD shook his head. "There wasn't a license plate on the car. And apparently it was the one time people were too stunned to pull out their phones. Other than the one shot that was on the news, there aren't any pictures of the car. And none of the driver."

Riley cried silently the rest of the way to the hospital. When JD pulled into a spot and dropped the car into park, she couldn't cry anymore.

They rode the elevator to the sixth floor, silent the whole time. Riley absently wondered if her parents knew she was missing, or if Hempstead and Gail the super sleuth had yet realized they'd been outsmarted by a seventeen-year-old girl.

They should have been protecting Shelby, Riley thought grimly. Although if it wasn't for her, her best friend wouldn't have needed protecting. Riley tried to swallow down the thought.

The doors opened on the sixth floor, and Shelby's whole family was crowded there. Worry and lack of sleep had carved deep grooves in Mrs. Webber's face. She bobbed one of the twins on her hip, gripping him with one hand, using the other to blot out the tears that seemed to leak from her eyes.

"Oh, Riley," Mrs. Webber said, handing off the toddler to another one of Shelby's siblings. "I'm so glad you're here."

She gathered Riley into a tight hug, pulling Riley against her chest until she was crushed against Mrs. Webber's T-shirt, smelling the comforting Webber house smells of crayons, tomato sauce, and cleaning products. The woman's body shuddered against Riley's, and Riley linked her hands over Mrs. Webber's back.

"I'm so sorry," Riley whispered.

Mrs. Webber broke the hug and stepped back, wiping her tears with the back of her hand. "Oh, I'm so sorry." Her eyes went to JD, standing quietly behind Riley. "I don't believe I know your friend."

Riley introduced them without making eye contact. "Is Shelby going to be OK? Can I see her?"

"Tru's in there now and Lily and George."

Riley thought of George Webber, a big looming brute of a man who wore a salt-and-pepper beard and called his daughter "my Shelby." A sob lodged in Riley's throat.

"I can wait."

"She's not family," Shelby's oldest sister said.

Mrs. Webber reached out and squeezed Riley's hand. "Yes, she is, Sara."

Sara's dark eyes seemed to focus on Riley and then narrow accusingly. Blood pulsed in Riley's temples, and she took a few stumbling steps backward, sure that Sara knew that the blue sedan—and this hospital—was meant for Riley and not Shelby.

"We'll just have a seat," JD said, threading his arm through Riley's and pulling her into one of the hospital's hard waiting room chairs.

"She's going to be OK," JD repeated, this time murmuring it into Riley's hair. His closeness—or maybe their distance from Shelby's family—seemed to break Riley's trance, and she suddenly dropped her face in her hands.

"I can't believe this. It's supposed to be me."

"No, Riley, it's not. It shouldn't have been anyone."

Riley heaved a sob. "But it's my fault."

"No, it's the guy in the blue sedan's fault." He rambled on. "So what were you doing before I picked you up?"

Riley knew it was JD's attempt at getting her mind off Shelby; it was something that her mother did when Riley had a panic attack: try to veer her off the subject of her panic.

Riley swallowed. "Um, I was—I was *not* packing my clothes."

"Well, that's good, considering you just moved into that house."

Riley nodded. "I know, but the FBI—"

JD's eyebrows went up and Riley stopped. What did people who were being forced to disappear say to their friends? *I was getting my things together because I'm going to be Greta VonSomething from Poughkeepsie, New York?*

Riley just shook her head. "It's nothing. Do you think we can see Shelby now?" She was out of her seat and moving toward the door when she came face to face with Tru.

Tru was Shelby's older sister and everything Shelby was not: tall, lanky, and oozing confidence. Her eyes flicked over Riley then went directly to JD.

"You came!" The waft of cold air that shot by Riley as Tru did sent goose bumps all over Riley's body. Tru threw her arms around JD's neck and hugged him close. Riley watched as JD's hands flailed for a half second before wrapping around Tru. She buried her head in his neck and JD drove his fingers through her long blond hair. Something stabbed at Riley. A tiny lick of anger started low in her belly.

Was she jealous?

Mrs. Webber poked her head in. "Ry, you can come see Shelby now."

Riley licked her lips and tried to breathe deeply as her hand turned on the knob to Shelby's hospital room. She opened the door, hit immediately with the smell of antiseptic and hospital-clean, her eyes adjusting to the dim light in the room.

"Shelby?" she whispered.

Her feet were planted just inside the doorway, and she jumped when Shelby's door snapped closed. Riley felt unable to move her feet forward. She felt smothered by the sterility of the room, like she had no right to be there, no right to grieve for her friend.

"Shel?" she asked again, this time taking a step, moving herself forward enough to peek around the curtain half-drawn around Shelby's bed.

Riley's heart dropped.

She shoved the curtain aside and raced to Shelby's bedside, trying to find some semblance of her best friend under the tubes and bandages and measures and beeps of the hospital equipment.

Shelby's face was almost completely covered in a thick layer of gauze. Its edges were tinged with rust-colored blood, dried against her skin. What wasn't covered was bulbous and ruined, scratches, bruises, and cuts made glossy by some kind of ointment. A ventilator tube was taped to her mouth and something else to her chest; tubes were held to Shelby's arm by thick needles. One was an IV; the other seemed to be feeding her blood. The blankets were tucked tightly around her torso, her one leg protruding, encased in an enormous cast, propped up by some kind of sling.

Riley felt the tears prick behind her eyes. Shelby's toes poked out of the cast, the ladybug pedicure that Riley had given her during their last sleepover badly chipped.

"I'm so sorry, Shelby," Riley said softly, her hand finding Shelby's among the bandages and tubes. "This is all my fault."

Riley gave Shelby's hand a gentle squeeze, trying not to focus on how limp and lifeless it seemed. "I never thought—if I had listened to you, none of this would've ever happened. You wouldn't be here." A tear rolled off the end of Riley's nose. "And now they want me to move."

The machine that monitored Shelby's heart beat along steadily, neither Riley's touch nor words making any difference.

"They're trying to make me leave," Riley continued, squeezing Shelby's hand again delicately, "but I'm not going to. I can't. Not with you like this." Riley sniffled, hoping to find her best friend somewhere underneath all this damage. "We're going to catch the guy who did this to you, Shelby, I promise you that. But you have to promise me something too. You have to promise to get better." Riley's voice cracked, but she went on. "Promise me. We're supposed to go to college together and share a dorm room."

In the back of her mind, Riley saw her parents sitting on either side of her, Deputy Hempstead explaining Riley's "new life."

"I'm not leaving you," Riley swore. "No matter what happens. But you can't leave me either. You just can't. You're my best friend, Shelby. Please, please wake up. I need you. I need you and I'm so, so sorry. I hope you can hear me."

She sat down in the chair next to Shelby's bed and pulled her knees up to her chest, hugging them tightly. "I'm staying here with you, Shelby, because you're going to be OK. It's kind of like one of our normal sleepovers, right?" She forced herself to smile. "Except this time you get the bed."

Riley rested her cheek on her knees, the steady beep of Shelby's heart lulling her to sleep, until the blaze of her cell phone cut through the relative calm of the room. She checked the readout: Dad's Cell. Her heart thudded as she sent the call to voicemail.

"I'm not going to disappear with them," Riley said, standing up and looking over Shelby again. "I'm not Jane Elizabeth. I'm Riley Spencer, and I'm not going anywhere."

Riley pulled the chair up against Shelby's bed and curled up in it, holding Shelby's hand until she fell asleep.

• • •

"Riley, Riley." Someone was jiggling her shoulder, and a flood of sunlight was stinging her eyes.

"What time is it?"

"It's six a.m."

Riley blinked and sat up, every muscle in her body aching. She blinked, the room—and her wake-up call—coming into focus.

"Mrs. Webber?"

She smiled thinly. "I came back in last night and you had fallen asleep. I didn't want to wake you. I think Shelby liked that you were here."

Shelby.

Riley jumped to her feet, the blanket Mrs. Webber must have pulled over her pooling on the ground. "Shelby?" Riley leaned over her friend's bed, her heart breaking all over again as she saw Shelby in the light now, the cuts and bruises looking more menacing, more devastating. "Did she—did she wake up?"

Mrs. Webber put a hand on Riley's shoulder. "No, honey, not yet."

Riley sucked in a sob.

"Why don't you and your friend go home now? You need to get ready for school. And please thank your parents for letting you stay here with Shelby last night. I tried to call but I must have the number to the old house. It kept saying it was disconnected."

Riley nodded, unable to speak. She kissed Shelby's hand and silently wished for her to wake up then hugged Mrs. Webber and stepped out into the hall. It was bustling and busy now, nurses race-walking past her, pushing carts and wheeling around IV bags.

Riley's mind raced. She'd have to get home. She pulled out her cell phone and her stomach dropped as the missed call register filled up her entire screen:

MISSED CALL: DAD CELL

MISSED CALL: HOME

MISSED CALL: DAD CELL

MISSED CALL: DAD CELL

It went on like that, until the very bottom of the screen. Back to back calls, just a few minutes apart.

"Let me guess: your boyfriend wants to know where you were last night?"

Riley's head snapped up. "JD! What are you doing here? Did you come back?"

He yawned and Riley noticed his rumpled hair, last night's clothes wrinkled.

"You stayed here last night too?"

"What did you think? That I was going to dump you here and then just leave you?"

Riley's surprise obviously amused JD, because a bright smile cracked across his face.

"I don't know—I guess."

JD just shook his head, his tone softening. "So how is she? Any change?"

Riley swallowed and saw Shelby's broken body in her mind's eye. She wasn't sure she'd ever be able to get that image out of her head. "Bad. No change."

"Do you want to stay here? I could go by your house and pick up some clothes for you or something."

Riley thought of JD driving up to her house, her parents, Gail, Hempstead, and whatever SWAT team he had hired pulling out their guns and throwing JD to the ground. "No, no, you'd better not."

She pulled her phone from her pocket and wiggled it, showing off the screen full of missed calls and messages. "I think I need to get home."

"I'm going to get a drink of water. Call and let them know we're on our way."

JD disappeared down the hall and Riley stared at her phone. She had never been frightened to call her parents ever before, but suddenly, she was paralyzed—and angry. If she went home, she'd be boxed up, stamped with a new name, and sent to God-knows-where. She'd never know when—or if—Shelby woke up.

"So, they call out the National Guard?"

Riley's stomach dropped. "What?"

JD strolled up behind her and glanced down at her phone. "Your parents."

"Of course they didn't call out the National Guard. They wouldn't do that. They're just regular. We're just regular people. Why"—Riley worried her bottom lip and dropped her voice to a low whisper—"why would you say that?"

JD looked around suspiciously then lowered his voice too. "Because I thought it'd be funny. Note to self: National Guard joke? Epic fail."

Relief—cold and sticky—crashed over Riley, and her heart started to thump at a normal pace again. "Right." She forced a laugh that was both too long and too loud. "Right. National Guard. That was funny."

JD's smile was quizzical. "OK…so, home?"

"Uh, no, actually." Riley held up her phone again as though it were definitive proof. "I called my parents. They're fine, you know, because I checked in. They just want me to help Shelby out."

JD shifted his weight. "OK, so are you going to stay here?"

Mrs. Webber poked her head around the corner. "Riley, why don't you and JD go out for a little bit? Maybe grab some sandwiches?"

Riley's stomach rumbled. She realized that since the few bites of half-solid spaghetti she had the previous night, she hadn't eaten. "Are you sure? We could just grab something at the cafeteria."

"I'm sure. It's not healthy to stay cooped up in here." She looked over her shoulder, her eyes traveling toward Shelby's room.

"Sure, Mrs. Webber."

FOURTEEN

JD leaned against the far wall in the elevator as they coasted downward. He looked Riley up and down. Her cheeks burned. "What?"

He shrugged. "I'm just surprised you don't have a problem with elevators."

Riley tried to look nonchalant. It wasn't that she didn't have a problem with elevators—it was that she had learned to control it. She remembered her mother's hand closing over hers.

"Come on, Riley. You and me, together."

Riley stared down at the threshold where the industrial gray carpet met the silver thread of the elevator doors' track. Her mother gave her arm a little tug and looked down at Riley—four or five years old then—her eyes soft and encouraging. Riley sucked in a deep breath and willed her right foot forward. She stared down at her glossy Mary Jane shoe on the floor of the elevator. And then the doors started to close. Panic rose and exploded across her chest, each finger of fear reaching out to pinch the air in her lungs. Her head throbbed and her eyes watered and her mother seemed so, so far away. Riley's hand was still in hers but the door was cutting through them, shoving Riley into a square metal coffin, tearing

her mother away from her. Locking her away. She could feel the walls
coming closer, could feel the cool metal brushing against her shoulders.

"*No!*"

Riley snapped out of the memory—the daymare—and offered
JD a tight-lipped smile. She laced her fingers and gripped her
hands tightly, watching the lighted numbers on the elevator door
click on and off until they reached the ground floor. Only then was
Riley able to breathe.

"OK," JD said when they stepped out of the elevator. "Where to?"

Riley opened her mouth and then closed it quickly. She squinted
through the glass double doors of the hospital. Heat pricked at the
back of her neck.

Deputy Hempstead was cutting a direct line to the front desk,
something pinched between his forefinger and thumb.

Riley's heart dropped into her shoes when the light caught it. He
was carrying her sophomore picture, now jabbing at it as he barked
at the woman at the desk.

Riley's hand clamped around JD's. She gave him a hard yank
back, the pair disappearing down a hall.

JD paled. "Was that the guy from the train station? Ry, what the
hell is going on?"

"Something bad, JD."

"Then we need to call the police. And I should take you home,
right now."

Riley just wagged her head, unable to answer.

"You didn't call your parents, did you? Look, Riley, usually I'm
all for ditching out and everything, but this guy has been following

you for a week. And from a different town. He could be dangerous. Do your parents know?"

Riley bit hard on her lip. "They don't care about me. They want me to move smack dab in the middle of my junior year. What kind of parents would do that?"

"Riley—"

"JD, if I go back home—or to the police—something bad is going to happen."

"You just said something bad *is* happening."

"I won't be here anymore. We'll have to leave."

JD frowned. "What do you mean, leave?"

"I can't really explain right now. Look, I get it if you don't want to be a part of this. Just do me a favor and don't tell anyone you saw me." She spun on her heel and speed-walked halfway down a hall before she felt JD's hand on her arm.

"Where are you going to go?"

She hadn't thought past avoiding a new life and a new identity. "I'm not sure yet."

"All right. Stay here." He guided her into a shadowed doorway at the end of the hall. "I'll go get the car and pull up at this exit. Just make sure no one sees you."

It seemed like hours passed while Riley waited for JD. When his car screeched up, she was finally able to breathe. JD barely waited for Riley to belt herself in before sinking his foot on the gas and glancing at her.

"I'm not even going to ask, Ry. You have to tell me what's going on."

"You're not going to believe it."

JD worked the muscle in his jaw. "Try me."

"I just don't want to get you in trouble."

JD's nostrils flared. "You probably should have told me that back in the bus bathroom."

Riley sucked on her teeth. "I'm not Riley Spencer."

"Who are you—007?"

It was a lame attempt at humor, and it died in the stolid air between them.

"I'm Jane Elizabeth O'Leary. That guy, the guy from Granite Cay? His name is Gavin Hempstead. He's a deputy U.S. Marshal."

JD seemed to push the car a little faster. "So you—were you kidnapped?"

"No." Riley shook her head and smiled at the thought—how much easier it would have been if that were the case. She'd never have to tell anyone; she could stay in her house, continue to be Riley Spencer. She cleared her throat and thought about how much to tell JD. But one look at his profile, one thought back to the way he showed up to take her to Shelby, and Riley started talking.

"My parents and I are part of the Witness Protection Program. I didn't even know until—" She tried to think back to that moment when her parents sat her down. It could have been two minutes or two months ago—her mind was in such a hazy fog. "I just found out."

"Are you serious?"

The phrase *serious as a heart attack* flopped in Riley's mind, but she stamped it down. Things were much more serious now. "Yeah. I didn't know—when I was looking up the birth certificate, trying to find information on the O'Leary family? I didn't know that was me—us."

"So then, do you normally have U.S. Marshals following you?"

There was a hard edge in JD's tone, and it struck Riley. "Are you mad at me? I didn't know—"

JD blew out a long sigh then was silent for a beat. "No, Riley, I'm not. I'm just"—he raked a hand through his dark hair—"I just didn't expect this—any of this."

She sank back against the bucket seat. "I didn't mean for any of this to happen."

"So, what happens now?"

Riley leaned her forehead against the cool window glass. "I have no idea. I think"—her throat was tight—"I think we have to disappear. Change our names again. My family and me, I mean."

"So that's what you meant by leave."

A sob choked in Riley's throat and she nodded.

"Do you have time for that bite?" What he didn't say hung in the air between them: *before they take you away.*

Riley rested her hand on her belly. "My stomach is in knots. I don't think I'll ever be able to eat again."

"OK, how about I eat and you hold down the other end of the booth?"

Riley tried to smile. "Sure."

They were silent on the drive, but Riley couldn't stop the voices in her head. What was she planning on doing? She couldn't run away from her parents. They had no choice: they were going to take Riley away.

Then came an inching, niggling thought: what if Tim was telling the truth?

Riley shook her head. She couldn't—wouldn't—believe a stranger over her own parents.

But her parents had lied to her for fourteen years.

JD clicked his blinker on right before turning onto a cracked driveway.

Riley glanced out the windshield and wrinkled her nose. "You want to eat here?"

It was a perfectly square restaurant, once painted a cheery tropical pink. The pink had faded and peeled and hung like bits of dead skin off the building, making its boring façade look less neglected and more zombie-homicidal. The neon "BU" of a once functioning *Burgers* sign twitched underneath lacy, fresh-looking curtains.

"Are you sure?"

JD skipped the regular parking lot and zipped around toward the back of the building, stopping the car just behind a fetid dumpster. Riley grimaced.

"You really know how to woo a lady."

JD chuckled. "Who says 'woo'?"

"Who parks their car five feet from a dumpster?"

"Someone who doesn't want his car spotted. The least I can do is give you a half hour of freedom."

Riley considered that and then nodded. "Good thinking."

JD pulled the door open and grinned. "After you."

Despite its faded, forgotten appearance, the restaurant was clean and cute inside: mismatched chairs surrounded light blue Formica tables, each dressed with a fake flower pushed into a milk bottle. It smelled homey—like butter and pancake batter—and Riley's stomach seemed to spring to attention, announcing that she wasn't nauseous; she was *starving*.

A redheaded woman who could have been Riley's grandmother pushed out from behind a swinging double door and grinned at them. She was big all around; she took up most of the doorway she was standing in. Her demure, faded pink uniform pulled against her chest and hung longer in the front than it did in the back. She matched the ensemble with thick white tube socks and a pair of gaudy black and purple Sketchers—the kind that was supposed to give your butt a lift. Riley smiled at the ground.

"Just the two a you?"

JD nodded and the woman opened up her arms. "I'm Rose. I'll be your waitress. Sit wherever you like."

Rose followed them to a corner table and laid down two enormous laminated menus then filled up two glasses with water and ice. Riley looked down at the menu, her stomach growling.

"Wow, this is a huge menu."

"Not really," Rose said, shifting her weight. "We're not serving any of this right now." She jabbed a finger, pulling it down the entire left side of the menu. "Or this. We've got bacon, no sausage, *huevos*, no *rancheros*." She laughed at her own joke, her apron jumping on her chest.

"How about burgers?" Riley asked.

"Oh yeah," Rose said. "We got those. Wouldn't have lit the sign if we didn't." She pointed her pencil toward the half-illuminated BU sign.

"Cheeseburger?" Riley asked. "Fries, Coke?"

Rose wrote it down, nodding at each word. "Check, check, and check." She turned her enormous boobs toward JD. "And for you?"

JD handed up his menu. "Same. But can you add bacon to mine?"

Rose narrowed her eyes playfully. "We got bacon. No sausage."

Riley leaned forward, feeling more comfortable. "Oh, and do you have cheddar cheese? Or just American?"

The smile fell from Rose's lips. "We got square cheese."

Riley raised her eyebrows and handed off her menu. "Good enough for me."

Rose disappeared through the double doors yelling "two cheesers!" to no one in particular while Riley pulled her tablet out of her purse.

JD's leaned in. "What are you looking up?"

Riley rested her elbow on the table, her chin in her hand. "You said you found Tim, Jane's brother."

"Your brother."

She looked up. "What did you say?"

"If you're Jane, then…"

"Not necessarily. Didn't you say you found some webpage? Where he was looking for…" Riley swallowed hard. "Where he posted stuff?"

"Yeah." JD slid the tablet to him and began searching.

Rose busted back through the double doors, Coke glasses in each hand. "So, what brings you two out today?"

"Uhhh." Riley and JD both started.

Rose tapped her finger against her lips and smiled. "Oh, I see."

Heat shot up Riley's spine, smacking the back of her head. "You do?"

"I'm no idiot." Rose's eyes cut from Riley to JD. "Young lovers, sneaking off."

Riley's heart pounded when Rose pointed to her.

"Your parents don't know you're out together, do they?"

"Yes, that's what we're doing. You won't say anything, will you?" JD said, his eyes going from nervous to sweet and imploring in one of Riley's thudding heartbeats.

"Oh, of course not. Who am I going to tell? It's just me and Mr. Tastee Freeze in here today. You all enjoy yourselves, and if you really love each other, that's what matters. Love conquers all, you know? That's what they say." She looked off. "Least that's what I think."

There was a ding from inside the kitchen and Rose jumped to attention. "Burgers are ready!"

JD watched Rose's back as she walked away. "Well, she's cheery."

Riley offered a tight-lipped smile and leaned toward JD.

"Have you found it?"

He frowned. "That's weird. I could have sworn it was on this site." He turned the tablet toward her. "It's not there anymore."

JD slid her tablet toward the wall, and Rose set down two enormous plates overflowing with double-fried fries and burgers with patties as big as Riley's head. The scent wafted up to Riley's nostrils and she couldn't remember ever being this hungry. She decimated every inch of burger and every single fry in what seemed like sixty seconds. JD pulled a fry through his puddle of ketchup and grinned.

"You eat like that around your boyfriend?"

She wiped the grease from her hands on her napkin and eyed JD. He had driven her out of town, accompanying her on this weird, unplanned hideout mission; he was skipping school; he was taking her safety into consideration.

Riley shifted her weight. "I need to tell you something."

JD sat up straighter, his eyes going saucer-wide. "Really? Something else? What are you—an alien? A Russian spy? A sister wife?"

She wrinkled her nose but smiled. "A sister wife?"

"It would probably be less crazy than a chick running away from some killer."

Riley shook her head. "No. It's just that I lied when I told you I have a boyfriend. I don't."

JD shrugged and crumpled his napkin onto his plate. "No big deal. Could be worse, I guess."

"How's that?"

"You could have told me you were an alien."

Riley crossed her arms in front of her chest. "And that would have been a serious issue?"

JD pinned her with a stare. "I have a very real fear of being probed."

"Noted."

They were silent for a beat. Then JD jerked his chin toward the phone in Riley's purse. "You should call your parents."

Riley chewed the inside of her lip, eyes glued to the phone's dark screen. She had turned the ringer off, but her parents—and

Gail—never stopped calling. There was even a text from Shelby's mom telling Riley to call home. She let out a long breath then went to dial. The screen illuminated then flipped instantly black.

"Battery died."

Riley felt slightly guilty—and slightly angry. She knew her parents were worrying. She knew she should just go home. *And I will, in a second,* she thought. But that little flame was there. They were going to pull her out of her *life.* They didn't even know if the Spencers were in any real danger, but Gail and Hempstead had already made arrangements.

She would never see Shelby again. They couldn't even text. JD would be gone too. She'd be at a new school. She'd be a new *person.* Tears rimmed her eyes and she wiped them on the sleeve of her sweatshirt. "Can you take me home now?"

JD nodded, and they both peeled a few bills, laying them on top of Rose's check.

When Riley pushed open the door, she was hit with a rush of cold air that shot goose bumps all over her body—but it wasn't the damp chill that made her teeth start to chatter. Her hackles went up.

"I feel like we're being watched."

JD scanned the parking lot. "There's not even another car around here."

Riley brushed her palms up and down her arms. "I can't explain it. I just feel like"—she turned around and around—"I just feel like we're not alone."

"Well, let's just get out of here."

JD made a beeline for his car and Riley was right behind him. She had her hand on the door handle when she turned back to the diner, the yellow lights flooding out through the window. Rose was standing there, arms crossed in front of her chest, her head cocked as she balanced a phone on her shoulder. Her eyes seemed to be fixed on Riley, her lips moving fast. Riley swallowed, her saliva sour and metallic—she was beginning to recognize the taste of her own fear.

FIFTEEN

Riley slammed the car door shut and JD sunk his key into the ignition.

"You ready to head home?"

Riley nodded, a thick lump in her throat. "Guess so." She paused for a beat, and then, "Can I borrow your phone?"

JD looked at her, brows raised. "Sure."

He handed the phone over, and Riley played with it absently before turning to him. "I need to call my parents. I've got to tell them everything, come clean, and whatever happens, happens. I mean, it's not like I can go out and track down this guy myself. The police aren't even able to do it." A heavy wave of sadness rolled over her. This was how it was going to be. And if someone found them in their new house, it would start all over again.

She dialed the phone while JD drove. He mouthed the word "gas" while she listened to the ringing of the phone.

"Hello?"

Riley bit her lip but pushed herself to speak. "Mom?"

"My God, Riley! Where are you? Where have you been?"

Her mother was sobbing, and guilt was twisting Riley's gut. She blinked back tears. "I'm sorry. I'm coming home right now."

"Riley Allen Spencer, do you know how worried we've all been? Deputy Hempstead and Gail have been working around the clock to find you." It was her father now, and he did nothing to hide the spitting anger in her voice.

Riley began to cry harder. "I'm sorry, but—"

"Where are you? Who are you with? Stay where you are, I'm coming to get you. I don't trust you to—"

"You don't trust me?" Suddenly, she stopped crying, rage tearing through her. "I wasn't the one lying for fourteen years! I'm not the one who is trying to force his daughter to *start* lying."

"We don't have a choice, Riley."

JD pulled into a gas station while she sucked in a sharp breath. "You have a choice. I don't."

Riley watched JD stuff the gas pump into the car then jog across the pavement into the tiny store.

"I'm sorry, turnip, but we can't take any chances."

She swallowed hard. "Don't worry. I'm on my way home."

She hung up the phone without waiting for her father's response then doubled over, holding her head in her hands. She blinked when something small and shiny caught her eye. It was embedded in the black car mat carpeting and she had to yank to get it out. She studied the silver charm in her palm, and her stomach soured.

The charm was broken.

She reached into her purse, her fingers closing around the

broken angel that the "squatter" had left in the house across the street. The two pieces, when pressed together, were a perfect match.

"Oh my God."

When Riley looked up, JD was at her window, holding a Coke out to her. His eyes skittered across the charm in her palm and went wide.

"You've been watching me."

Anger, fear, and hurt welled up inside her. She blinked back tears. "You—"

Riley went for the door handle but JD snapped the door shut again.

"You don't understand. Just stay there and let me talk to you."

She started to shake her head, her hands splayed as she pressed against the door. "I don't want to talk to you. Let me out, JD."

His lips inched into a mean grimace and his nostrils flared. "You have to trust me."

We asked you to trust us…

A damn of hot tears broke and washed over her face, silently dripping over her chin. Everyone begged her to trust them, and everyone lied to her.

JD pushed back against the car door, his dark eyes challenging. Riley edged back on her seat, moving toward the driver's side, and JD was around the car like a shot, pulling open the driver's side door.

She shuffled the other way.

Riley felt the wisp of wind as JD reached for her, his fingertips grazing her hair as she kicked open the passenger's side door and, once her feet made contact with the cement, took off running.

"Riley!"

The desperate way he screamed after her made her sick. She heard the echoes of the man from the mall, the man from the train station, Gail, and her own parents saying her name, ordering her back, wrapping her in their lies.

Riley cleared the cemented gas station and went for the grove of eucalyptus trees that butted up against it. Each time her foot fell, she heard the crush of dried leaves, the pop of twigs. The menthol scent of the grove stung at her eyes and she palmed the tears away, scanning for someplace to hide, for some way out of the grove and into safety.

"Riley, please!"

JD's voice was behind her, barely clipping at her ear.

"I'm on your side!"

She wanted to believe him. She wanted to stop running. She had wanted to stop running just after this whole thing began. She had gone from being sheltered Riley Spencer with a completely normal life to a shadow named Jane, constantly on the run, constantly looking over her shoulder.

"Riley!" JD's voice was fading as Riley covered more ground.

She ran until her muscles hurt, until she was sure JD was gone. She dropped to her knees, feeling the moist earth dampening her jeans, and cried. She couldn't trust anyone. Her best friend was in a coma, and everyone else in her world was lying to her.

JD had been *watching* her. She felt herself shudder. Was JD working for someone? Was he being paid to watch her? Had he known she was Jane all along? The thought made her whole body ache. He wasn't a friend; he was a spy.

For who?

Riley willed herself forward, and after a few steps, her heart sped up when she began to hear the whooshing of cars racing by. The eucalyptus trees were thinner and sparser here, the grove opening up to a sidewalk on a quiet, suburban-looking street. The houses were old but well-kept with manicured lawns and pretty pots overflowing with flowers. The calm scene almost made Riley feel safe.

She stepped out of the forest, focusing on a pot of bright red roses directly in front of her. They were the last thing she saw before everything went dark.

• • •

Everything hurt when Riley woke up. Her shoulders, her stomach, her legs—everything felt heavy and bruised, and her mouth burned with the bitter taste of bile. And it was dark.

Her whole body started to move, to roll, and she instinctively put out a hand and a foot to steady herself—or she tried to. Her legs were bound together at the ankle, a thick ring of duct tape encircling her legs halfway up her calves. There was duct tape around her wrists too, and Riley started to panic.

Where am I?

Her eyes weren't adjusting to the overwhelming darkness until flashes of red, one by her head and one by her feet, illuminated just enough of Riley's surroundings for her to make them out.

Black, industrial grade carpet. The faint smell of gasoline. The rumble from underneath her.

A car! My God, my God, I'm in someone's trunk!

Her mind immediately went to JD, and she cringed, her stomach turning over. *He wouldn't do this to me, he wouldn't do this to me…*

The silver charm flashed in her mind. The image of a dark figure standing in the window, staring down at her. JD.

She gritted her teeth and refused to cry, instead, using her bound feet to kick anything and everything she could reach.

"Help!" she screamed, and struggled against the duct tape, but the more she did, the more it burned hot rings into her skin. "Help!" she screamed again.

The car started rolling again and Riley quieted, trying to listen for any sound—a radio squawk, a police siren—but all she heard was the constant flow of traffic.

What had they told us to do?

Riley had sat through a half-dozen school assemblies about safety and stranger danger and how to run away. *Had there ever been one about being locked in someone's trunk?*

She started kicking again, screaming, and trying to use her fingers to claw at the roof.

Nothing happened. The car kept rolling.

After what seemed like a lifetime, Riley felt the car turn onto a road that wasn't as smooth as the other. The car bounced around, and she bounced in the trunk, wincing, completely unable to protect herself from the next blow.

And then the car stopped.

Everything inside her went hot. She didn't want the car to keep moving, but once it stopped—right now—she would be faced with

JD. He had drugged her, duct-taped her, and tossed her in the trunk. What was he planning on doing with her now?

She heard a car door slam and the sound of footfalls on gravel. She knew they were drawing near. Her heart thumped with every step, but she couldn't breathe.

Her bladder felt heavy as she heard the jingle of keys and then the smooth way they slid into the lock. She used every last muscle she had to scooch herself to the darkest corner of the trunk, her back up against something hard and metal.

"Please, JD," she whispered. "Please don't hurt me."

She couldn't help it; she clamped her eyes shut when the trunk opened.

"I didn't want to have to do this. I didn't want it to turn out this way."

Riley opened her eyes and stared into Tim's ice-blue ones, which looked as sharp as ever. She started then pressed herself tighter, deeper into the depths of the trunk. Tim reached out and grabbed her bound ankles and slid her forward as if she didn't weigh a thing.

He grinned down at her before pulling her out of the trunk and slinging her over his shoulder. "I told you that you don't have to be afraid, Janie. I told you I'm the good guy in all this."

Riley knew she should be screaming. She should be struggling or banging on Tim's back with her bound hands, but she was paralyzed by fear. She wanted to believe that Tim was a good guy, but good guys didn't snatch girls off the street, bind their limbs, and toss them in the trunk.

Her throat was bone dry, and all she could do was hang there listlessly as Tim carried her up a cement walkway. She stared down at the concrete as he pushed a key into a lock and, after stepping inside, dropped her on a couch.

Riley looked around, startled. The couch was sagging and full of holes. The room smelled musty and earthy, as if every window was open. It was dark, but Riley could hear Tim moving around, and little by little, snatches of the room were lit up as Tim lit candles all around her. He finished with a Coleman lantern which was in what Riley supposed was the half-rotted kitchen.

Once things were sufficiently illuminated, Tim stood in front of her with a wide grin. He threw his arms wide. "We're home!" he said, as if Riley was a willing participant.

Riley cringed on the musty couch, trying to find her voice. "Why are you doing this to me?"

Tim's proud smile dropped. "Why am I bringing you home?"

"This isn't my home. I don't live here."

"It's only because it's been so long since the last time you were here. Could have been longer but you changed all that."

Riley blinked. "*I* changed that?"

Tim pointed to Riley and then to himself. "You were looking for me. I had alerts on my computer. You accessed the Granite Cay databases and searched Jane Elizabeth O'Leary. I thought it might just be a random hit but…" He shrugged, rolling up onto his toes like they were sharing a giddy reunion story. "But it was you!"

Riley's mouth was suddenly bone dry. "How did you know it was me?"

"I traced your Internet for a while, but it had been so long I couldn't be sure. I had to see for myself, so I came out to see you."

"At the mall…"

"No." Tim swiped at the air as if she had just said something silly. "I was watching you for a long time before that. You look so different."

"You—you were in my house?"

He actually looked sheepish. "I gave you the postcard at the carnival, but you didn't respond. I had to go inside."

Riley's whole body went heavy. "So you came to Crescent City because of me. I—I did this?"

"It was like a homing beacon. And then to find that you were only in the next state! Do you know how happy I was?"

The Witness Protection Program had only moved us one *state away?* Riley fumed. It didn't seem logical. In the movies, they moved families halfway around the world, or into nondescript tract-home communities. *Tim said they were lying. Tim said they would have made stuff up.*

Riley tried to shake off the inching doubt as Tim rambled on.

"Once I found you, I knew there wouldn't be a lot of time. That's why the house—our house—doesn't look as nice as it used to."

"Our house?" Her eyes darted around the room. The house was clearly a tear-down, because sheets were tacked to the walls, little gusts of wind sucking the fabric through gaping holes. The floor was covered in garbage, dirt, and wood debris; there was a broken lamp tossed on a pile of scorched wood where the floor bowed. In the one spot that didn't look about to be demolished was a small aluminum table with two chairs—rusty but workable. There was a small vase with a couple of mums stuffed in, and behind that, broken shelves were littered with cereal boxes, a loaf of bread, peanut butter, and jelly.

"You live here?" Riley asked.

Tim pointed to her and then to himself. "*We* live here. You're my sister, remember?"

"I'm not your sister." She tried her best to inject confidence in her voice. "Let me go, please."

Tim looked down at her with an appraising expression that made Riley even more uncomfortable.

"Let me go." She felt her strength and anger growing. "LET ME GO!" She twisted toward the dark, greasy window at her side and thumped her bound hands against it, trying to reach it with her feet.

"Help! Help!"

The toe of her sneaker caught a crack in the glass and she was able to kick through. Joy obliterated her fear and she screamed louder, a string of tear-choked nonsense words.

"Please help me! Someone, please, he's crazy, please!"

Tim just stared down at her until Riley, covered with a thin sheen of sweat, stopped screaming. She flopped back hard on the couch, tears rolling from her eyes and into her ears.

"No one can hear you. There's no one around here. The neighborhood is mostly abandoned. Except for us." He smiled as if that were a good thing. "I can't believe I found you. You look so much like Mom did when she was younger."

Riley gritted her teeth. "I'm not your sister. We're not siblings. I don't even know you!"

A dark expression cut across Tim's face. "Don't say that. You are." He advanced on Riley, pulling a small blade from the food shelves.

Riley pulled her knees up to her chest, trying to make herself as small as possible. Her whole body was shaking. It didn't even slow Tim down. He grabbed her by the arm and brandished the blade then slit the duct tape down the center.

"But you have to promise me you'll be good," he said, pointing at her with the blade of the knife. "You have to listen to what your big brother tells you."

Riley's ears were ringing. "You're not—"

Tim whirled and stamped his feet. "Do not say that!" He looked like a child, his apple cheeks flushed a deep red, his eyes wild and unfocused.

He's crazy, Riley thought.

She swallowed hard. "I was just going to ask you, how am I supposed to know you're my brother? Where have you been all my life?"

Tim's nostrils flared. "They left me. They left me like garbage, just like they're planning on leaving you."

"I—"

"I'll prove it!" Tim raged.

He yanked her up and plopped her down in one of the aluminum chairs then wound a length of duct tape around Riley's torso and arms. He held his finger to her. "Once you believe me, I'll take that off. If you're good."

Riley blinked. Tim's cadence and behavior swung from normal to almost childlike in a matter of seconds, and the switch was chilling—both sides Mr. Hyde.

She heard Tim tinker with some things behind her, and her mind started spinning. He was behind her with a knife. She couldn't see what he was doing, had no idea what he was thinking.

She had to get him to free her. She had to find a way to get loose. Her eyes went to the rectangle of window that wasn't covered by a sheet. She squinted, seeing nothing but darkness and the foot-sized hole she kicked through. Where were they? How long had they traveled—how long had she slept?

"There!" Tim dropped a large manila envelope on the table in front of Riley. He snatched it up again then upturned it. "Proof."

Riley watched as pictures floated out of the envelope. "I don't understand, Tim. What are these?"

One of the photos worked itself free from the envelope and floated down. It landed face up directly in front of her—an answer to her question.

The bottom fell out of Riley's world.

She recognized the scene immediately—the birthday party from the postcard she received. But in this one, everyone was ready, grinning and facing the camera. The boy, dead center, eyes round and focused on his cake.

And Riley's mother next to him.

SIXTEEN

Everything was a blur. Every thought, image, or memory she had shaken, false, wrong.

"That's my mother," Riley whispered.

Tim shuffled a few more pictures around then dropped another in front of Riley. It was the same scene, and he jabbed at it. "Dad." His eyes cut to Riley and there was a crazed, pleased look in them. He jabbed again. "You."

Riley leaned closer, scrutinizing the photo. She, her mother, and her father were all in this one. She, a toddler in a fluffy pink party dress, sitting on her father's arm.

And Tim was right between them.

"That's you?"

He nodded. "That was my ninth birthday. Mom made a coconut cake. You threw it up on your dress."

Riley felt exposed, the intimate details of a past she didn't even know laid out for her on a cheap aluminum table by a complete stranger.

"This is when you were smaller. We were all at the zoo."

Another picture of this unknown happy family. Riley, a bald-headed infant, was reclining in a stroller. Tim, younger, but very much the same kid, grinning a toothless grin, his hand firmly held by Riley's father while giraffes stood in the background.

"Do you remember this Christmas?" Tim pushed another snapshot in front of her. "You got a tricycle. I got a fire truck."

A vague memory unhinged itself. Riley, small, being placed on a shiny red tricycle. She felt her father's hand on the small of her back, giving her a gentle push. She could smell the fresh pine, and somehow knew that her mother was making noise in the kitchen, just off to her right.

Riley swung her head, her eyes scanning the debris pile then trailing back to what remained of the kitchen. "This was our house."

Tim did a little happy jump. "That's what I've been trying to tell you, silly!"

Riley's head started to throb. This was the house Jane Elizabeth O'Leary came home to after she was born at Granite Cay Hospital. They were in Granite Cay! It was a little more than a six-hour drive from Crescent City. Riley's eyes ticked with moisture. Who was going to find her now? Would Gail, Hempstead—would her parents even think to look here?

"You're surprised, aren't you? I knew you would be."

"What happened to it?"

Tim looked away, his shoulders slumping. "I tried to fix it up nice for you. But when you left, there was no one to take care of it. Homeless people came and tried to stay here, and the city tried to tear it down. I tried to make it nice though."

"Wh—what happened to you?"

His eyes were hard again. "They took me away."

"Who's 'they'?"

Tim gritted his teeth. "The people my parents left me with when they disappeared."

There was a tightness in Riley's chest. Why didn't she remember Tim? Had her parents really left him? She didn't want to believe it, but the evidence was scattered all around her. Riley cradled in her mother's arms at the beach while Tim dug sand in the background. Her father and Tim, locked mid-arm wrestle.

Proof.

Her parents had left him behind. Tears clouded her eyes. She wanted to tell him he was wrong, that her parents would never do that, but the truth was she wasn't sure she knew what her parents would do. She didn't know who her parents were anymore. Nadine and Glen wouldn't leave a child behind, but maybe Seamus and Abigail would.

"They didn't tell you where they were going?"

Tim swung his head. "I was asleep."

"And they left you here?" Riley gaped.

Who were these people?

"I was sleeping in my other house. The house where they put me."

Riley wasn't sure what to say. "So you gave me the postcards."

Tim nodded. "But you didn't do what I told you."

"You said my parents weren't who I thought they were. You said you knew who I was."

"And then I came and found you. You were supposed to leave them and come with me. You were supposed to know what the postcards meant."

Riley looked away. "You didn't sign them or anything. How was I supposed to know who they were from? How was I supposed to find you?"

Tim sighed. "I was there, Janie. I was there with you the whole time."

The pleased look on his face turned Riley's stomach.

"Oh." Tim clapped. "You must be hungry." He went to an ice-packed cooler and picked something out. "I got you something special. Hot dogs! I remembered you love them."

Riley couldn't remember the last time she ate a hot dog. When her parents changed her name, had they changed everything else about her too?

Her pulse raced as Tim set a pot on an ancient hot plate and filled it with water. He stared down into it before dropping the hot dogs in.

"What do you want from me?"

"I don't want anything from you, Janie. But I had to save you. Your parents are awful, awful people. Taking you away from them will teach them a lesson."

Riley dragged her tongue across her chapped bottom lip. "You know they didn't have a choice when they left."

Her father's sullen voice, telling Riley the same, hummed in her ears, and she missed her parents terribly. They wouldn't disappear while she was here, bound to a spindly aluminum chair—would they?

She didn't want to look at pictures anymore. She didn't want "proof," didn't want any more creeping memories of life in this broken-down house. She had to get out, even if it meant getting on with her life should her parents abandon her.

Tim set a hot dog on a paper plate in front of Riley. He pulled out the chair across from her and sat down, his own plate in hand. She watched him pick up a hot dog and take a huge bite, juice dripping over his filthy fingers, his lips smacking as he ate. He gestured toward her untouched plate.

"Aren't you going to eat?"

There was no way Riley could sit across from this stranger, in the midst of this dirt and debris, and share a meal. She was about to say the same when a thought struck her.

"I can't." She tried to shrug her shoulders and the tape puckered with a tight sucking sound. "I need my hands to eat."

Tim gazed at her, considering. "You're going to be good, right?"

Riley nodded, keeping her eyes focused on Tim's.

"'Kay."

His fingers wrapped around the knife, and she tried not to look afraid. He slit the duct tape, and Riley's whole body fell forward, blood rushing to her arms, shooting pins and needles. She waited for Tim to put the knife down while silently judging the distance from her chair to the front door. The house was small, much smaller than the Blackwood Hills one, but she'd have to cut in front of Tim to get to freedom.

It was worth it.

The door hung slightly lopsided on the frame, the bottom cracking with water damage. There was a lock that looked new, but she was sure a swift kick would knock the whole thing off its rusted hinges.

"Where—is there a bathroom here?"

"I've been working on it for a month now. It even has water. Do you remember where it is?"

Riley shook her head. "I don't remember."

Tim pointed toward the pile of debris. "You go right behind that and there's the hall. It's the first door." He grinned. "Your bedroom is the second."

The thought of her sleeping in this house, with him there, sent pricks of anxiety all the way through Riley. She gritted her teeth and forced herself to breathe deeply, to focus—anything to quell the unease that was welling inside her.

"Thanks."

She pushed her chair back and stood slowly, certain that the thundering of her heart would set Tim off. He waited for her to stand then went back to finishing his dinner. Riley took one glance at the top of his head as he ate, and when the adrenaline surged through her, she took off running—or tried to.

Her feet were still bound.

The duct tape loosened up a tiny bit, but Riley was going down. Her body hit the moldy, dirty floor with a thud, and the wind was sucked out of her. But Riley refused to stop. She clawed at the ground, wriggling toward the door, her fingers digging into the floor. She felt the wood splintering at her fingertips, the old, dead wood pricking into her flesh. It hurt, but Riley didn't care. She only wanted out.

"What are you trying to do?" Tim was standing over her, his body blocking most of the light in the room, throwing Riley into a dark shadow. "What are you doing?"

He was angry. As he yelled, spittle came out of his mouth and Riley thought about that night in the housing development—the car, the high beams, the man pounding on the sliding glass door and demanding she come out.

"That night." Her chest was tight and sweat pricked out at her hairline and upper lip. "That…" She gasped, trying to suck precious air into her lungs. "Was…" Every word stabbed at her. "You."

"You weren't listening to me! Just like now." Tim crouched down, his face a few inches from Riley's. "You're not listening to me!"

She was in full panic attack mode now, struggling to breathe as black streaks swirled in front of her eyes. Her head felt light but her temples pounded and she couldn't remember what the doctor had told her to do. That seemed like lifetimes ago, anyway.

"What is wrong with you? Stop that! STOP THAT!"

But Tim's proximity and his yelling was only making it worse. "Stop!"

His hand sliced across her shoulder and connected with her cheek. She heard the smack of his palm before she felt the sting.

Everything stopped.

"You're as bad as they are," Tim spat, his voice low. "I don't think I can trust you. Now don't move or I'll—I'll have to…" His eyes flicked from her face to the floor behind her head. "Don't you move or I'll have to do something bad."

The tears were pouring from Riley's eyes as Tim stamped around the room, grabbing things from the shelf. He poured something on a towel and came at her with it. She tried to struggle; she used her arms to push him away, but he was strong and easily overwhelmed her, pinning her arms down and sitting on her chest. He pressed the cloth against her mouth and nose before she could protest, before she could scream. And then everything went dark.

• • •

Yellow-white sunlight poured over Riley's forehead and she squinted, trying to block it out. Her head was throbbing to an angry, insistent drum beat, and she felt like she had been sleeping for days.

A little wiggle of something gleeful erupted inside of her. JD. Tim. Hempstead and Gail. It had all been a dream.

She opened her eyes, blinking away the fog and sleep then focusing on the blankets that covered her. The coverlet was cream-colored and smattered with delicate pink roses. She was in a single bed with a cheap white arching footboard. It stood out against the mildew-gray walls and the few remaining streaks of faded green wallpaper. Where was she?

It all came flooding back in a hideous filmstrip, and Riley pulled her knees to her chest, wrapping her arms around her legs and gently rocking. Fear fueled every cell, and she was almost too terrified to move, thinking that somehow, if she could stay perfectly still, she could fade away, ooze into the mattress, disappear. Her fingertips grabbed the fabric of her pants and she frowned, realizing that she was in a pair of knee-length flannel pants with ruffles around the hem. The shirt she wore, sleeveless with a baby-pink polka-dot pattern, matched the pants.

It wasn't the pajamas that scared her—it was the fact that someone had put her in them. She started to breathe heavily again, to feel the sharp edges of another panic attack coming on, but she refused to allow herself to focus on that when there were much bigger issues at hand.

Where was she?

Where was Tim?

Did her parents even care that she was gone?

There were slippers placed under the bed for her, and Riley grimaced as she slid into them—they were her size, exactly, but nothing she would ever pick out. The swirly pink and purple pattern was too girly and young, something a child might like.

Because Tim had shopped for his little sister.

Riley would have thought she was numb to the cold, nauseous feeling that thinking about Tim shopping for her gave her, but it was back again, full force, and she felt the urge to heave. She stamped it down and picked her way carefully across the half-decimated floor, refusing to consider what made the gnawing little holes in the floorboards. She pressed her ear against the door first and, hearing nothing, slowly turned the knob.

The door was locked.

She jiggled the knob then pounded the door, kicking it with her slippered feet. "Tim! Tim! Let me out of here!"

There was no response on the other side of the door, and Riley rushed to the small window above the bed. She refused to call it "her" bed. The window was narrow and long, with slits of light pouring in through the boards tacked haphazardly on the outside wall. There was no screen on Riley's side, and most of the window glass had been shattered, but the boards crossed out any opening bigger than Riley's ring finger.

She turned back to the room, her eyes scanning for anything that could help. The remains of a white dresser were useless, the cheap pressboard crumbling in her hand. The closet doors had been removed and the graffiti in the closet cavity had been hastily painted over. There were only three hangers in the closet, and new clothing, tags still on, hanging on each one. There was a pair of stiff jeans, a long-sleeved shirt, and a short-sleeved one. There were packages of thick white gym socks, panties, and sports bras in a bag on the bottom of the closet, and set carefully next to that was a pair of knock-off gray Converse in Riley's size, seven and a half. She shuddered thinking of Tim, wondering what he said when he shopped for her. Did he mention they were for the sister he was planning on stealing?

Her clothes—the clothes she had come in with last night—were nowhere in the room. Neither was her purse. But she wasn't going to dwell on that. She grabbed the package of socks and shoved a pair on then slid on the sneakers. She refused to touch anything else Tim had bought for her, but she needed the shoes for traction. She gripped the pole the clothes were hanging on and yanked with all her might. It bowed and the wood groaned. She shimmied it from side to side and one side broke through the wall. She was able to yank the thing down then, coming with it, landing with an "oof" on the wood floor.

She heard running footsteps then and the lock tumble on her

door. She quickly shoved the pole back in the closet and jumped back into bed, pushing her sneakered feet under the covers and clamping her eyes shut.

Riley heard her door open. Her whole body went stiff when she heard Tim's shuffling feet come closer. She could feel his hot breath, heady with the scent of strong coffee, brushing over her cheek as he leaned down toward her. He put his hand on her head, and it took everything Riley had not to shirk away, not to cringe as he stroked her hair.

"I'm so happy that you're home, Janie. We're going to have so much fun together, just like we used to. I saved you from them, Janie. They are very, very bad people."

Riley mashed her face into her pillow and bit down hard on her bottom lip. She felt her teeth slip through the skin and tasted her own blood, but it was the only way she could keep her mouth shut. Inside, everything was trembling. Inside, everything was fighting him, was reaching back to her parents, begging their forgiveness.

Please don't leave me, Mom and Dad. Please don't leave me here with him.

SEVENTEEN

Tim sat at her bedside for a few minutes more before Riley felt his hand go to her shoulder, gently shaking it.

"Wake up, sleepy head."

She opened one eye carefully, worried that if she tried to pretend to sleep anymore, Tim might do something awful to her. She blinked and he smiled.

"Are you hungry? I got us breakfast."

Riley tried out her voice, unsure if she could still speak. "I need to go to the bathroom." She thought of Tim taking her clothes off and sliding on the stiff new pajamas, and her skin started to itch. "Can I take a shower?"

Tim cocked his head. "You're not going to try to run away again, are you?"

"No." She swung her head. "No, I won't, I promise."

Tim scrutinized her then slowly stood and went to the closet. "What happened here?"

He looked over his shoulder and Riley shrugged. "Old house, I guess."

Tim picked up the clothing, mercifully not looking for her shoes. He set the jeans and the short-sleeved shirt on Riley's bed. He pointed to the bag. "There are underthings in there. I'll go get you a towel."

A tiny flicker of something like hope rose in Riley's chest as Tim left the room, leaving the door open. She rushed to it, wracking her brain, trying to remember what Tim said last night. Her bedroom was the second door from the bathroom, and the bathroom was right off the hall. She could make it to the living room. She could make it out the front door.

Riley crept to the doorway and swept the hall, relief crashing over her when she didn't see Tim. She took the first step, her sneaker brushing over the threshold, her eyes focused on the open bedroom door at the end of the hall. She turned, silent as a mouse, and ran directly into Tim.

He held a big yellow towel out to her. "The bathroom is right there. I'll wait here for you to finish." He pointed to a spot right outside the door.

"Can I close the door at least? I would feel uncomfortable…"

Tim pumped his head. "That's OK. I'll still wait here."

Riley slipped into the bathroom, closing the door on Tim. She was grateful to find an old-style slide lock, and she slipped it into place. She didn't know if it would hold, but just seeing a locked door—locked on her side, not his—made her feel safer. Riley surveyed the decent-sized bathroom. It was surprisingly cleaner than the rest of the house. The tile floor was cracked and dated, but it was free of the garbage and broken wood that littered everywhere else. The toilet was hideous with a cracked seat and bits of rust, but it seemed to actually flush. There was no shower curtain on the bar above the tub, but there was a fresh bar of soap by the sink.

Riley checked the door a second time then checked every inch of the bathroom, looking for a weapon, a cell phone, a key—anything that would help her, anything that would fan the flame of hope struggling inside her.

But there was nothing.

The small window to the left of the toilet was a good six inches above Riley's head, and even when she stood on the toilet, she could see that the heavy, swirled glass was rusted into place. Even if she could open it, there was no way her body would fit through.

She didn't want to shower. If she was going to die here with her psychopath of a brother, there really wasn't any point. But her skin was beginning to itch from the dirt and dried sweat, and she forced herself to turn on the tap, to strip off the foreign clothes.

She stood under the chintzy flow of lukewarm water and rubbed her hands over the soap. Tears started to fall as the clean, spicy smell of the suds filled the bathroom. It was the same way her father smelled—the same soap he used.

"I'm going to get out of here," Riley muttered under the clattering sound of running water. "I'm going to get out of here no matter what it takes."

She rinsed her body and her hair as best she could under the weak stream then wrapped the thin towel around herself. She shoved her bare feet into the sneakers and opened the door. True to his word, Tim was there in the hall, sitting on the floor. He was eating a donut, the pink box propped in front of him. "You want one?"

Riley was starving. Her stomach let out an embarrassing growl and she nodded. Tim handed the box to her and she picked a donut out, eating the whole thing in two bites right there in the hallway. He shook the box again and she snatched another one, vaguely wondering if they were drugged but not caring as the thick, doughy thing hit her stomach. Her mouth was coated in sugar but she took a third donut anyway, eating this one more slowly as her stomach caught up to her brain.

"You were hungry. Maybe we should go somewhere for lunch."

Riley stiffened. "Go out?"

"Yeah."

Riley's heart started to pound, and suddenly she felt light and airy, even with a quarter pound of donuts weighing her down. If she could get out of this house and into civilization, she could get away.

She nodded. "I need to get dressed first."

"We'll go in a little bit."

She took a tentative step. Then, "Where are my clothes?"

"They're in your closet."

"No." She shook her head. "My clothes from before."

"You don't need them anymore. You don't need anything from before anymore. You have new clothes. And a new house, and a new life!" Tim smiled. "A new old life." He shooed her away. "Go inside and change."

Riley went into her makeshift bedroom and pulled the packages of underclothes from the bag. She slid the bra and panties on and shimmied into the jeans—they were stiff and a little baggy, but they would do. She pulled the long-sleeved shirt over her head and put her feet properly in the sneakers.

Then she pressed her ear against the door.

She could hear Tim whistling to himself in the other room. Then she heard him flick on a radio, settling on a news station. She turned then was sucked back to the door when she heard the radio lady start, "Still no word on the Crescent City girl who went missing yesterday morning. Police are still holding a school friend of the girl's, but he hasn't been charged yet."

Riley's throat tightened. She felt a nagging pain for JD then remembered the broken charm, the way he chased after her, screaming her name.

He could rot in there, Riley thought, peeling away from the door. *But I'm not going to rot in here.*

She picked up the clothing pole from the closet and wrapped her towel around one end. She used the toweled end to push the rest of the glass out of the window, then pressed hard against one of the wood slats, praying that it was as old and rickety as the rest of the house.

"Janie, are you ready? Come out here!"

Tim was knocking on her door.

"One second!"

She dropped the pole down on her bed and balanced herself on the metal headboard. She could feel the cool wind from outside sweeping over her face, reddening her cheeks. But the pole hadn't budged the board tacked over the window. So Riley did the only thing she could think of. She pulled the sleeve of her new shirt over her hand and picked up a shard of the broken glass. Even through the cotton shirt, she could feel the sharp, mangled edge. She slid it in her pocket and jumped off the bed, going for the door at the same time Tim opened it.

"What took you so long?"

Riley kept her shoulder against the door so he couldn't push it open any wider.

"Nothing," she said, winding a hand through her wet mess of hair. "I was just looking for a hair tie."

"You used to always wear it in pigtails."

Riley wanted to tell him to stop. She wanted to tell him that he had no right to those memories, no right to images of her and the things she did. Instead, she shoved her hands in her back pocket, running her index finger lightly over the glass in her pocket.

She followed Tim out the front door and stopped cold when she saw his car in the driveway. The front left bumper was scratched and smattered with dings, and a small crack spider-webbed across the bottom of the windshield.

"You—you—"

She couldn't say the word. She couldn't say "You hit Shelby" without tearing the glass shard from her pocket and going for his neck. But if she did that, even on a surprise attack, he could easily overpower her, and even if she did get away, where would she go? The few houses that looked lived in were set well back from the road, well back from this house. There were vines and overgrown shrubs everywhere, but he knew what was out here; she didn't.

Tim opened the car door for her and she slid in, sitting gently to protect the glass. Once he shut her door, she slid it from her back pocket and into the front. Riley's stomach roiled when the car engine rumbled. Her saliva was sour, and she fought back angry tears, not caring when Tim hit the door lock button and she was trapped inside.

"So you've been watching me a long time then?"

"Not that long. Only a few weeks, maybe a month now. You weren't easy to find."

"So you stayed around Crescent City?"

He nodded, turning away from the old-fashioned looking sign that said, *Granite Cay Downtown Historical District—Food! Shopping! Fun!*

"Why aren't we going that way? It said 'food.'"

Tim shrugged her question off. "There're too many people downtown." He poked Riley in the ribs. "I don't want someone stealing you away again."

Bile itched at the back of her throat. *No one is going to find me here. No one is going to rescue me.* She thought of her parents, of never being able to see them again.

"I thought you said they were going to leave me."

Tim's jaw stiffened. "I don't trust anything about those people."

Would they even come for her? She gritted her teeth. Deputy Hempstead had found her here once; he would find her again. *Right?*

"Did someone help you?" She thought of JD, her stomach starting to quiver. "Did someone help you find me?"

"No." Tim swung his head as he guided the car toward a bank of strip malls—and passed them. "What do you mean?"

"There is a boy," Riley started, shocked at what she was sharing. "His name—his name isn't important. He lives—was living—across the street from me. He watched me."

Tim frowned. "I know that boy. He wasn't helping me. He wanted to hurt you."

"What?"

"I was at your house one time. I was looking into your windows—just to make sure it was really you, Janie, and he was there too. He yelled at me. He told me to go away because he didn't want me to help you."

Riley blinked, confused. "JD chased you away?"

"He didn't want me to help you."

She looked out the window, silent, until Tim pulled into the parking lot of a small restaurant, set aside by itself on the outskirts of town.

"Ready?"

He kept a hand clamped around Riley's upper arm, guiding her into the restaurant. "Remember, if you act up, they're going to take you away again," Tim murmured into her ear as the waitress led them through the nearly empty restaurant. "They'll make you disappear."

He squeezed her arm a little harder, and Riley nodded, the pain making her even more determined to never get back in the car with Tim, to never go back to that awful house.

Riley scanned the menu without reading anything on it. Instead, she checked everything in her peripheral vision, anything to use as a weapon, any way to slip out of the restaurant and out of Tim's grip. There was nothing. She could just start screaming, telling everyone her story, but she was terrified that Tim would clamp down on her, overpower her, and rush her out of the restaurant.

When the waitress came, Riley mumbled an order, studying the wall behind the waitress's black bouffant.

That's when she saw it.

Tucked away on the other side of the restaurant: a fire alarm.

No one responded to calls of "help" or "rape"; your best bet is to yell "fire."

While the waitress was taking Tim's order, Riley broke in. "I need to use the restroom, please."

Tim cut his eyes to her, his expression fierce, but he couldn't forbid Riley from going without the waitress finding it strange.

She pointed her pencil. "Right down there, hon."

Relief washed over Riley. The walk to the bathroom took her directly past the fire alarm. Riley made a beeline for it and, feeling a spark of adrenaline in her arm, reached out and yanked the thing.

Her heart dropped when nothing happened.

It must have taken a second, maybe more, but it seemed like ages before the fire bell clanged. It was deafening and people were looking around, confused.

That's when Riley dashed into the ladies room, closing the door behind her. She moved a garbage can up against it—it wasn't much, but it would slow someone down—and looked frantically around the restroom. Her heart almost bounded out of her mouth when she saw the window above the sink. For the first time in what seemed like decades, she smiled, and the tears that poured out of her eyes were happy. Riley hopped up on the sink and cranked the old-style window as wide open as it would go then popped off the screen.

Her fingers ached as the metal window frame dug into her skin, but with the cool wind hitting her face, she didn't care. The toes of her sneakers scraped against the cheap stucco, and within seconds she was half out the window, halfway to freedom, on her way back to Crescent City. She didn't care about the way the metal dug into her ribs as she shimmied her way out, clawing at anything she could reach. There was cement below her, and with the way her body was angled, she would have to move out headfirst.

It didn't matter.

She gave herself a final launch and felt her hands—first one and then the other—scrape the concrete. One arm gave way immediately and she heard a pop then felt wave after wave of white-hot, blinding pain surge from her shoulder to her fingertips. But she was free.

She was behind the restaurant now, and from the corner of her eye, she could see patrons ambling around the front door, looking confused as the fire-bell continued to clang. She heard sirens in the distance, but they sounded far off. Riley weighed her options—she could wait for the fire truck and tell them her story but chance running into Tim. Or she could run now.

It wasn't even a thought.

Once Riley righted herself, she cradled her left arm in her right and took off running, wincing at the pain in her shoulder, relishing the sound her sneakers made as they slapped against the concrete, putting distance between herself and Tim.

Riley had no idea where she was going, no idea in which direction to run. All she knew was that she had to get away from that restaurant and get away from Tim. But he wasn't dumb. The restaurant sat alone among empty storefronts or businesses that only operated on weekdays. Riley cleared them all and kept running.

When she heard the hum of an engine after twenty minutes of jogging up to CLOSED signs and empty windows, she slowed, panting, relieved. The pain in her shoulder was overwhelming, and simply moving was zapping her energy. When the car pulled up alongside her, she broke down into a raging, primal scream.

Tim stopped the car, opened the passenger side door, and swept her inside.

EIGHTEEN

Riley, curled into the bucket seat, watched the stern set of Tim's jaw as he continued down the road. He didn't say anything to her, not even when he picked her crumpled, wailing body from the sidewalk and dropped her in the car. He would grind his teeth, the motion making the muscle in his jaw flex. His nostrils were flared, and rage marked a red path over his forehead and cheeks.

"You shouldn't have done that," he said finally.

Anger pricked through Riley, and all at once, the searing shoulder pain momentarily stunted. She was too mad to be afraid.

"You shouldn't have done this," she spat, each word punctuated, each word its own sentence.

Tim swung his head toward her, his expression a sickening one of pure innocence.

"What was I supposed to do, Janie? I know you don't believe me, but they were going to leave you. They were going to hurt you. I couldn't let them leave again. I couldn't let that happen."

He gripped the wheel harder, his knuckles going white.

"I couldn't let that happen," he repeated.

Riley dropped her head in her hands, hopelessness creeping though every vein. Her shoulders slumped and now the pain was everywhere, wracking her entire body. He was going to win.

She thought of Shelby then, small and broken in her hospital bed. "You hit my best friend. You hit her and tried to kill her."

Tim slammed on the brakes, and Riley was flung forward, her ribcage screaming out as it slammed against the dashboard.

"I did that for you! I did that so you would understand and get a clue! They were all out to get you!"

The red went all the way to the tops of his ears, and he was breathing hard, fisting his hands and slamming them against his head as he spoke. "I don't know why you won't believe me! I have to make you see! You have to know I was right!"

Terror, cold and heavy, crept through Riley. She could feel a rivulet of blood dribbling over the lower lip she bit. She watched the blood drop, forming a perfect circle of velvet red when it dropped onto her shirt.

"I don't believe you." The voice that came out of Riley's mouth— calm, determined—wasn't her own. It was confident—it was mad. "You're crazy."

Tim turned to her, fire burning in his eyes. His lips were slightly parted in a snarl that contorted his whole face into something terrifying. Slowly, he reached for Riley, going directly for her bad shoulder. His hand closed over her delicate limb and he squeezed, effortlessly, the pain ruining her.

She screamed and he released her, shoving her against the car door with a simple flick of his wrist. Tim pushed the car back into drive and drove, eyes focused straight ahead, a low, eerie whistle seeping from between his puckered lips.

Riley was silent, cradling her arm as Tim slowly took the turn that led to the house.

She would die before she went back to that house.

Tim tapped the wheel with his fat fingers, whistling along to a song that only he could hear. Riley breathed deeply before launching herself across the cab. Startled, Tim's hands went to his face.

But Riley's went to the steering wheel.

She turned it in any direction it would go and kicked at the gearshift. It was only a split second before Tim regained his composure, one hand going for the wheel, the other grabbing Riley's hair, but the damage had already been done. The car lurched and groaned; every light on the dashboard flashed before going out completely.

"You bitch!"

The car was aimed directly at the house, and Riley scrambled out of Tim's grasp. She could hear each hair as it broke in his grip, her scalp burning. She screamed and kicked against him, biting at the hand he tried to clamp over her mouth.

He didn't care.

His fingers moved over her chin and settled on her neck, squeezing, crushing at her windpipe. She was struggling to breathe. Her body, thrown into panic mode, was desperate for air—just like a panic attack.

Riley tried to stay calm. She took a short, shallow breath when his grip momentarily loosened, and it was in that moment of clarity that she heard the sirens.

Lord, please don't let it be in my head.

Tim's head snapped up and she knew it wasn't.

He scrambled for the door, one hand still tangled in Riley's hair, the other still clamped around her neck. He slid her right out with him, Riley struggling to gain her footing as he went for the walkway.

"Freeze!"

Tim stopped, his hand tightening around Riley's throat. Her vision started to fade, even as the siren sounds became stronger.

They're not going to make it…

Somewhere, in her periphery, Riley heard car doors slamming, but Tim was still pulling her.

"Riley Spencer!"

Tim switched his grip from her throat to her waist, propping her up like a rag doll. Her arms were pinned to her sides. Riley heard the rustling then the slick sound of a blade slicing air before the cold steel was pushed against her flesh. She saw the glimmer of the blade just under her right ear.

"Stay back! I don't want to hurt her but I will! I won't give her back to you alive. I won't! I promised her I'd keep her safe! She's better dead than with them!"

Riley's stomach curled in on itself. Even when she saw Deputy Hempstead coming up the walk, she didn't feel safe.

He had both hands splayed, his eyes locked on Tim's.

"I need to know that Riley is OK."

"I don't know who Riley is," Tim spat. "I'm just bringing my sister home." He dug his fingers into Riley's flesh, and she squeaked, her eyes damp with tears.

Riley's teeth started to chatter. She was going to die. Tim was going to kill her and she was going to die.

She wanted to die.

The pain was all around her, throbbing, tearing, pulsing. She thought of her parents, the house in Crescent City, Shelby's heap of a car. She absently wondered what name they would use on her tombstone.

"Janie's not your sister, Timmy."

Riley's head snapped up, all thoughts of death shot away.

Her father was coming up the driveway, was just over Hempstead's left shoulder. His eyes crested over Riley, heavy with apology, but his gaze set on Tim.

Riley could feel Tim stiffen.

"What are you doing here?"

"I'm sorry, Timmy, we both are. We shouldn't have left you."

"See?" Timmy was speaking to her now, shaking her with every word. "I was right. They left me. They're going to leave you too!"

Riley looked to her father, who had stepped in front of Hempstead and was almost close enough to touch. She could see her mother behind him. She shook off Gail's grip, and Riley saw that Gail held a gun, pointed at the ground. Behind her were three squad cars with officers taking aim.

"You need to let her go, Timmy," her mother pleaded. "You know that, don't you? Please let her go."

"She wants to be with me. We're home. This is our home. I told Janie the truth about you two. I told her how I went to sleep and when I woke up, you stole her and you just disappeared. You left me like I was nothing."

"You had a family, Tim."

"No!" Tears were streaming down his face. "You were my family!"

Her father raked a hand through his hair. "We spent a lot of time together, Timmy, and we loved you. But you were free when Alistair was arrested. They made arrangements for you to go home and live with your parents again."

"We didn't want to take you away from them."

"No."

Riley's mother pushed her way to the front. "We loved you, Timmy—we still do. But you had a family to go back to and we had to leave. We couldn't take you from them, especially after Alistair already had. We didn't have time to say good-bye. But we knew you'd be back with your parents soon."

"My parents didn't want me back. They wouldn't take me back. They *sold* me to Alistair. They knew what he was doing. You were going to save me." He was heaving now, tears and snot dribbling over his lips. "You promised you would save me!"

Riley could see her father visibly pale. "We didn't know, Timmy. We didn't know."

"They took me to live with strangers! You left me and you took away Alistair and I had nobody. And you still had her!" His words were dripping with spite. "You took her and not me!"

He shook Riley hard, and she could feel the blade saw against her skin a little more. Her emotions were crashing all over her. Pain, relief, anger. Her parents really did know Tim. They really did leave him behind, and now he was here, holding a knife to her neck in front of a house that she didn't even remember.

"It wasn't like that, Timmy, honestly."

"Stop it! Stop it! You're lying. You're lying and Jane knows it. She hates you! She hates you like I do. Tell them, Jane. Tell them!"

He tightened the blade against her skin, and Riley could feel the fibers beginning to split. "Tell them," he commanded.

"I don't want to."

"Tell them!"

Riley looked at her mother then her father, the tears rolling down her face, flopping from her chin. "I hate you," she whispered.

He shook her so the blade scraped against her skin. "Say it so they can hear it. So they can hear it and they'll leave us alone."

Riley tried to look at the ground, but all she could see was Tim's filthy hand, gripping the blade that was pinching at her neck.

"I hate you," she said louder. "I hate you." She thought of Shelby, of her own terror, of all that had happened. Her blood was liquid fire. "I HATE YOU!" Riley grabbed the shard of glass out of her pocket, not caring when it sliced into her flesh. "I hate you," she screamed, sinking the glass into Tim's thigh.

He howled, his hands scrambling to get a grip on the glass, and Riley ran.

She was shivering when she reached her parents. Her teeth were chattering, and all the pain from her injuries crashed together at once as Gail and the police pushed ahead of them, advancing on Tim.

"I don't hate you," Riley was crying. "I don't. Please don't leave me behind."

NINETEEN

Riley picked at the tape spread across the back of her hand.

"He was just a kid—nine, ten. According to Alistair, Timmy was his grandnephew. He was the youngest by far, and occasionally, he would come home with Mom and me. We were like a little family in some respects, but we always knew—or thought—that he had a family back in Ireland. And Alistair…"

Mrs. Spencer piped in. "When the deputy marshal came for us, we tried to take Timmy, but we had no legal grounds to. We had to go into hiding and he was someone else's kid. It broke our hearts, but it was the right thing to do. The government assured us he was out of Alistair's reach and would be on his way back to his family."

Riley looked up at her parents and frowned. "I almost feel kind of sorry for him. He had all these pictures of us together, and he was living in our old house."

"There's something wrong with him, turnip. But he's going to get the help that he needs."

Riley looked away, her eyes flitting over the bouquets on the desk. There were at least a half dozen, some done up in Hawthorne High colors, others with cartoony cards begging her to get well soon. They were from friends she would never see again.

"So, when do we leave?"

Mr. Spencer took Riley's free hand and patted it softly. "Tomorrow, probably. Maybe as early as tonight if all goes well."

Riley blinked back tears. "OK."

"Turnip! I thought you would be happy to get out of here and go home."

"Home where?"

He squeezed her hand. "We're not going anywhere, Ry. Not for a long, long time."

She sucked in a breath. "What are you talking about?"

Riley's mother stepped forward, hugging her elbows. "When you went missing, we had to put an all-points bulletin out. It—you— were just too important. We weren't going to listen to what the marshals said. We needed to get you back." She smiled softly.

"It worked like a charm! Alistair stuck his neck out."

"What your father is saying is that Alistair turned up, and the FBI were able to arrest him."

Riley's stomach started to flutter. "Like, forever, or just for a few months?"

Her father nodded. "The charges are going to stick, turnip. We don't have to hide anymore. We can't! Your face has been plastered on every television screen and telephone pole in a sixty-mile radius."

Riley narrowed her eyes. "You didn't use a dumb picture, did you?"

Mr. Spencer grinned down at her. "The dumbest!"

She was about to respond when the hospital room door burst open. "Hey!" Shelby, dressed in a flimsy hospital gown and wheeling an IV, stood in the doorway, gaping at Riley in her hospital bed.

Riley's father jerked a thumb over his shoulder. "Did we tell you Shelby is feeling better?"

"Come on, Glen," Riley's mother said, threading her arm through his. "Let's give the girls some time to talk."

Riley felt slightly uncomfortable seeing her parents in the doorway. "You're leaving us alone?"

Her father shrugged. "You're attached to an IV. How far can you go?"

Shelby hopped up on the end of Riley's bed then wriggled over for a hug.

"I was so worried about you! I mean, after I woke up I was. But my God, with medical technology what it is, you'd think they could have woken me up or patched me in or something."

Riley just laughed at her friend.

"Nothing exciting ever happens here. And when it does, I'm in a freaking coma."

"Shelbs, there is nothing medical technology can do for you when you're in a coma—you sleep like the dead anyway. I practically have to use a blow horn to wake you up after trig."

Shelby produced a SweeTart from somewhere and popped it into her mouth. "That's only because trig is a natural sedative."

"And you know what? I would have gladly traded places with you and slept through this whole lousy ordeal."

Shelby held her thumb and forefinger a half inch apart. "It wasn't even the teensiest bit exciting?"

"If you call being stalked by a guy claiming to be your brother exciting."

Shelby puckered her lips, pouting. "I guess not. But what about JD? Wasn't he, like, your partner in crime? I mean, only after I was otherwise indisposed."

Riley swallowed hard. She hadn't thought about JD since she'd been admitted and wasn't sure she wanted to now.

"I don't know about, JD, Shelbs. I thought he was my friend, I thought he was on my side. But…"

But what had Tim said?

"Well, you can ask him which side he's on then fit him for his Team Riley jersey right now."

"What?"

Shelby pointed to the long glass window in the door, where JD was pacing outside, a huge bouquet in his hand.

"I thought you hated JD."

"You see a lot of things differently when you've had a near-death experience, Ry. JD might be a good guy. I might be in love with a male nurse."

Riley rolled her eyes when Shelby hopped off the bed and sauntered out of the room, her IV squeaking along behind her.

Riley heard JD and Shelby exchange pleasantries then his head popped through her door.

"Do you mind if I come in?"

Riley shifted in her bed. "No, it's OK. Come on in."

JD stood at the foot of Riley's bed, the two silent for a beat. Finally, JD held the flowers up. "I got you these," he said, as if he just remembered them.

Riley couldn't help but smile. "They're beautiful."

"I don't have a vase or anything." He paused, considering. "Riley, I wasn't—"

"Spying on me? I know, and I'm sorry. Everything was just so—"

"Yeah, I know and—"

"Right. I—he—Tim…" The name was bitter on her tongue. "He mentioned that you were there. Watching him while he was watching me. You chased him away."

Pink washed over JD's cheeks and he looked at his feet. "I rang the doorbell. Not exactly the most heroic of actions."

Riley shrugged then immediately winced. "That's still sore. As for the bell ringing? Whatever works, right? It distracted him."

"But he still got you." There was genuine sadness in his eyes, and Riley softened.

"So how did you end up in the house across the street?"

JD grinned. "Changing the subject to get my mind off losing you? That's my tactic."

There was a little flutter in Riley's stomach when he said the words "losing you," but she chalked it up to the green Jell-O they'd been shoving down her throat rather than anything else.

"So?" she asked.

"I was—I was living in that house."

"What? Why?"

"My foster family kicked me out. I turned eighteen a few weeks ago, remember? No more kid, no more checks."

Riley struggled to sit up. "You don't have foster parents. You said yourself, your parents have baby pictures of you all over the house."

JD suddenly became interested in Riley's wall of flowers. "Wow. A lot of people love you, huh?"

Riley grabbed his shirtsleeve. "JD."

He turned and offered a shy smile. "Wishful thinking about the wall of pictures. I never really knew either of my parents. Lived with my gram until I was five; then it was foster care after she died."

She nodded.

"I didn't know you lived in that neighborhood when I got there, honestly."

"But you had binoculars."

JD swallowed hard. "I saw you when you were leaving for school one day. I realized it was you, not just some girl."

Riley tried to remain calm. "So you got the binoculars to stare at me specifically?"

"No. I was skipping school, hanging out in the house, and I saw a car stopped in front of your place. It came after both of your parents left, and sometimes the guy would park there at night too. He was watching you."

She nodded, that nauseous feeling in her stomach again. "Tim."

"Yeah. I wish I would have called the police or something."

Riley forced a smile. "Remember that for next time."

"I'll try to remember that." He cracked a half smile, but it immediately fell away. "So, when are you going?"

Riley felt her brows rise. "Going?"

He studied the palm of his hand. "To be someone else. Somewhere else."

She let out a long breath. "Um, I'm not."

JD looked up, and this time he was smiling. "You're not?"

"The one bright spot in trying to get me and my parents killed was that it brought out Alistair Foley, the guy who was after us."

"Alistair Foley?" JD looked impressed. "I read about that online. That case was huge. That was the guy who was after you?"

Riley nodded. "Yeah, my dad used to work for him. My parents put my picture all over the place when I went missing. Apparently, he saw it and thought it would be a good idea to be part of the chase…or something."

There was a slight lump in her throat. Her parents had risked their lives to get her back. They had given up their location and plastered Riley's face in public—after spending fourteen years in hiding. Alistair came out because of her—he came after her parents because of her. She felt her eyes starting to water.

JD's hand found hers. "Hey, you OK?"

"Yeah, yeah. Just—I don't know, medication side effect or something."

JD nodded, sitting next to Riley on the bed. "I'm really glad that you don't have to disappear again. Well, I'm really, really glad that you get to stay Riley Spencer."

"Really? Why's that?"

This time JD looked directly at her, lacing his fingers through hers. "Because I think I really, really like her."

EPILOGUE

Riley Spencer and her kidnapping were old news. People whispered about the Spencers being in the Witness Protection Program but no one really believed it, and Riley was completely OK with that.

"It's almost dinnertime, turnip," her father said, poking his head into her room.

Riley smiled. The nickname "turnip" had never sounded so good. "I just need to start this paper, Dad. Then Shelby, JD, and I are going to go to the mall. I might bring Bryn from across the street."

Her father cocked an eyebrow. "Four of you at the mall at this hour?"

Riley rolled her eyes. "It's barely six and we're going to a movie."

"I guess I can talk your mother into that."

"There's no imminent threat anymore, Dad. You can loosen the reins."

"It's still my job to keep my turnip safe."

Riley groaned and tossed a stuffed animal into the doorway her father just vacated. She pushed aside the framed picture of her parents chasing her as baby Riley—one or two at the most—took off on her tricycle.

She opened her laptop and started her paper:

My name is Riley Jane Spencer. I live in Crescent City, California, with my mom, who wears horrible, holiday-themed turtlenecks, and my dad, who does the worst impression of Jimmy Stewart ever. They are overprotective and completely embarrassing, but they're my parents, and I wouldn't have it any other way.

ACKNOWLEDGMENTS

First and foremost, many thanks to my brilliant editor Leah Hultenschmidt who knew how to get the best out of me with this one. Cat Clyne, Derry Wilkins, and the rest of the Sourcebooks gang, I couldn't have found a better home—thanks for welcoming me. Amberly Finarelli, my incredible agent—we're back together and now all is right with the world! Thanks to my family for their continued support, especially my brand new nephew Lowen Scott who had nothing to do with this book, but is irresistibly adorable.

I can't even begin to thank my best friend and constant support, Marina Adair, for listening to my plot problems, being my nurse because I'm a klutz, and checking in during deadlines to make sure I'm not dead. Joan Wendt, it all started with you and I plan to make good on every bar tab and Hawaiian vacation you've ever picked up. To the Rogue Writers: we're one step closer to conquering the world!

ABOUT THE AUTHOR

Hannah Jayne is possibly the only person living in Silicon Valley who has never worked in high tech. When she's not writing, she's obsessively watching HGTV or shopping at Target, also obsessively. Find out more about Hannah's urban fantasy, young adult thrillers, and latest obsessions at www.hannah-jayne.com.

CHECK OUT MORE YA THRILLERS
FROM SOURCEBOOKS...

TRULY, MADLY, DEADLY

Hannah Jayne

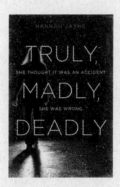

THEY SAID IT WAS AN ACCIDENT...

Sawyer Dodd is a star athlete, straight-A student, and the envy of every other girl who wants to date Kevin Anderson. When Kevin dies in a tragic car crash, Sawyer is stunned. Then she opens her locker to find a note:

You're welcome.

Someone saw what he did to her. Someone knows that Sawyer and Kevin weren't the perfect couple they seemed to be. And that someone—a killer—is now shadowing Sawyer's every move...

PRAISE FOR *TRULY, MADLY, DEADLY*:

"A fast-paced thriller." —*Kirkus Reviews*

"What a ride! Full of twists and turns—including an ending you won't see coming!" —April Henry, *New York Times* bestselling author of *The Girl Who Was Supposed to Die*

BROKEN

CJ Lyons

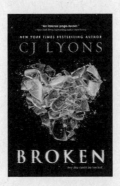

ALL SCARLET KILLIAN WANTS IS A NORMAL LIFE.

Diagnosed with a rare and untreatable heart condition, Scarlet has come to terms with the fact that she's going to die. Literally of a broken heart. It could be tomorrow, or it could be next year. But the clock is ticking…

All Scarlet asks is for a chance to attend high school—even if just for a week—a chance to be just like everyone else. But Scarlet can feel her heart beating out of control with each slammed locker and vicious taunt. Is this normal? Really? Yet there's more going on than she knows. And finding out the truth might just kill Scarlet before her heart does…

PRAISE FOR CJ LYONS:

"Everything a great thriller should be—action packed, authentic, and intense."
—#1 *New York Times* bestselling author Lee Child

"Laurie Halse Anderson's *Speak* meets Kathy Reichs's *Virals*."
—Jill Moore, Square Books, Jr., Oxford, MS

SIX MONTHS LATER

Natalie D. Richards

SHE HAS EVERYTHING SHE'S EVER WANTED— BUT NOT HER MEMORY...

When Chloe fell asleep in study hall, it was the middle of May. When she wakes up, snow is on the ground and she can't remember the last six months of her life.

Before, she'd been a mediocre student. Now, she's on track for valedictorian and being recruited by Ivy League schools. Before, she never had a chance with super jock Blake. Now he's her boyfriend. Before, she and Maggie were inseparable. Now her best friend won't speak to her.

What happened to her? Remembering the truth could be more dangerous than she knows...

PRAISE FOR *SIX MONTHS LATER*:

"Filled with tension and heart-in-your-throat suspense that kept me guessing to the very end." —Jennifer Brown, bestselling author of *Hate List* and *Thousand Words*

"This smart, edgy thriller taps into the college-angst zeitgeist, where the price of high achievement might just be your soul." —*Kirkus*